"Yes, I'm emotional," Emerald said.

"Because I'm never going to know. I'm never going to know what it could have been. I'm never going to know what passion is. Not really. I waited, all this time. I've never been kissed, I've never been touched, I've never—"

Andrei kissed her. He could take it no more. He swallowed her words down like the sweet honey that they were, an elixir that turned his dark soul into sunshine as the sweetness of her mouth flooded him. He kissed her because he could do nothing else.

He kissed her, because he wanted her. Because he had wanted her all this time. She clung to him, her fingers pushed through his hair as she deepened the kiss, as she parted her lips and slid her tongue against his, as she arched her body against him, her breasts firm against his chest.

"Please," she whispered. "I didn't promise to be a virgin bride. I don't want to go to his bed untouched. I want to have *you*. One night. Please."

He gripped her hips and growled. "No."

"Andrei—"

"Why should we light ourselves on fire only to burn? Don't you see? This is going to kill us both."

Enjoy this thrillingly dramatic royal trilogy by Millie Adams!

Young, Hot and Royal

Regal, reckless and in need of a ring!

You're cordially invited to the most outrageous royal wedding season of all!

Princess Emerald causes a scandal when she's kidnapped from the royal altar by her bodyguard... and father of her secret baby!

Enjoy the drama of *Princess, Pregnant, Prisoner*

Available now!

Marrying merciless King Lucian might be the most dangerous decision of Lilith's life, until she realizes she's falling for her captor...

Get swept away by *King's Captive Bride*

Palace maid Birdie shares an incognito night with brooding King Onyx...only to discover she's secretly pregnant with the royal heir!

Don't miss Birdie and Onyx's story

Both coming soon!

PRINCESS, PREGNANT, PRISONER

MILLIE ADAMS

Recycling programs for this product may not exist in your area.

ISBN-13: 978-1-335-21373-0

Princess, Pregnant, Prisoner

For questions and comments about the quality of this book, please contact us at CustomerService@Harlequin.com.

Harlequin Enterprises ULC
22 Adelaide St. West, 41st Floor
Toronto, Ontario M5H 4E3, Canada
www.Harlequin.com

HarperCollins Publishers
Macken House, 39/40 Mayor Street Upper,
Dublin 1, D01 C9W8, Ireland
www.HarperCollins.com

Printed in Lithuania

Millie Adams is the very dramatic pseudonym of *New York Times* bestselling author Maisey Yates. Happiest surrounded by yarn, her family and the small woodland creatures she calls pets, she lives in a small house on the edge of the woods, which allows her to escape in the way she loves best—in the pages of a book. She loves intense alpha heroes and the women who dare to go toe-to-toe with them.

Books by Millie Adams

Harlequin Presents

The Forbidden Bride He Stole
Her Impossible Boss's Baby
Italian's Christmas Acquisition
His Highness's Diamond Decree
After-Hours Heir
Dragos's Broken Vows
Promoted to Boss's Wife
Heir of Scandal
From Convent to Queen

The Diamond Club

Greek's Forbidden Temptation

Work Wives to Billionaires' Wives

Billionaire's Bride Bargain

Visit the Author Profile page
at Harlequin.com for more titles.

CHAPTER ONE

"So, it's to be a loveless marriage, to a stranger in a strange land."

Princess Emerald of Basilia stared up at her older brother, King Onyx, his gaze dark and uncompromising as it ever was. And then to his left, at her brother's right-hand man, and her bodyguard, Andrei Ardelean.

He might as well have been carved from stone. He was a man who exhibited little emotion, unless you knew him. And Emerald and Onyx were two of the very few people who knew him. Sometimes, Emerald could even get a smile out of him. But not today.

"If you wish to look at it that way, Onyx," she said, staring her brother down, her rebuttal to his attempt at making her decision sound unhinged obviously irritating him.

"It is not how I *wish* to look at it," he said. "It is how it is."

"And what other *solution* do you see? King Lucian asked for me."

King Lucian, ruler of Alabria, The Sea Serpent of the Mediterranean. The most feared, loathed and reviled ruler in the string of islands that made up the Jewel Belt.

"You are my sister, you are not a political bargaining tool."

"Sadly, Onyx, I am. That's what it means when you're born into royalty, and you know that. We have to do what is best for the country. There is no other choice."

"There are many other choices."

"King Lucian is liable to bring his fleet of ships to our island and raid the place to take me."

Andrei shifted where he stood, his black gaze menacing. "He is welcome to try." Even after all these years of living in Basilia, he retained hints of a Romanian accent.

His parents had been fleeing a crime family, so the story went, and they had stowed away on a boat bound for Basilia, but it had sunk and they'd drowned.

Andrei was the only survivor.

He'd washed up on shore, and it had been her mother's and father's natures to take him in like he was their own. That poor, lonely orphan had become a symbol of the welcoming nature of their country. But she knew it had never really been about that. It was about love.

It was only after that that her father and mother had been killed in a car accident, and her brother Onyx had ascended the throne at the age of sixteen. Andrei had been part of the family by that point. Onyx had appointed him as her personal bodyguard, and so he had become her shadow, wherever she'd gone. The three of them were bonded together by loss. By trauma, and she could understand the pushback from them now. But both of them were far too pragmatic to behave this way.

They weren't *children.* Not anymore. They had to put away their fantasies of this place, being separate from the world and being their own personal haven.

They knew better than that. Onyx knew better than that, whatever he said. He himself was in a loveless marriage with a woman who didn't care for him at all. Emerald and Andrei both hated to see it, and Onyx wouldn't hear a negative word against his queen. Because he had chosen her for reasons of diplomacy. Nothing else, and that mattered to him more than anything. She understood that it was hard to watch your sibling take less than what they deserved, but she also understood why he'd done it. Ultimately, she respected him for it, because he was serving a greater need, a greater good.

That he didn't see her as worthy of doing the same spoke to the fact that however much he tried to pretend that he saw her as an equal, he didn't. It infuriated her. They were royal, they had a duty to their country above all else. Above all notions of love, passion or even personal happiness.

Her mother had given up everything she'd ever known to marry her father, and that marriage had united a kingdom.

How could Emerald do less? In honor of a mother who was no longer here, but who had shaped her in every way that mattered?

She decided to tell him as much.

"What's good for you is good for me. What's good

for the future of the country is what I must do, just as you did when you married Circe."

"Don't speak ill of my wife. Do not compare her to a maniacal authoritarian."

"The rumors about King Lucian are simply that. Rumors. We don't know that he killed any of his wives."

"Even if he killed one of them, it's a wife too many. And anyway, they seem to always meet an end, don't they."

"There were only two. He's hardly Bluebeard."

"And this also isn't *A Thousand and One Nights*. You're not going to be able to tell him stories and keep him from doing what it is homicidal maniacs do."

She decided to ignore her brother's hysterics. She'd already reasoned out all of this. She'd been going over the logistics of an alliance between their countries for the past year. She'd first made contact with King Lucian six months ago, via email, and while he was difficult and mercurial she didn't think he seemed like a psychopath.

Though, maybe good psychopaths hid it well. She couldn't know for sure, and she felt it didn't benefit her to be complacent, but if she really felt that she was signing herself up for murder she wouldn't be doing it.

She believed him, ultimately, that what he wanted was an alliance.

Alabria was isolated, had very few alliances with anyone, and would make an excellent trade partner and military ally.

It was just that Lucian wanted marriage in exchange for those things.

She was a good negotiator. She always had been. She could think of no reasonable excuse to deny him what he was asking. There would have to be a better political prospect on the table, and currently, there wasn't.

So she'd agreed to the marriage.

It was signed. Notarized. Official.

Onyx's objections to it meant nothing.

Legally.

They meant something to her personally. But what she wanted personally wasn't the feature here.

She was a princess. With that came an obligation to duty and legacy. That was what mattered to her.

"The agreement that he sent over is very reasonable, and does not have a hint of homicidal ideation. The fact of the matter is, this is a great proposition, a boon for our country, and you know it."

"I don't like it. In fact, I would like to forbid you from doing it."

"Don't. We agreed that I wasn't going to be treated like I was inconsequential because I was younger, and a woman. I am one of your key political strategists and have been for years. I am not your spare, Onyx."

"Of course not. You never have been."

"Then let me do this. Alabria is the gateway to the Jewel Belt of the Mediterranean. Being able to move through that route freely would change the economy of our country. Alabria is bigger than we are. *He* is more powerful. I know you don't like to admit that there is any man on earth more powerful than you, but there is a point where ego becomes foolishness."

His lip curled, his offense apparent. “This is not about my ego, it is about your safety.”

It was only then she let herself look at Andrei. His eyes burned bright with a sort of black flame that made her feel a world of things she didn’t want to feel. That made her feel…

There was regret in taking this marriage offer, of course. There were so many things she hadn’t done. So many things that she wanted that… They were impossible, and they always would be.

There was, in addition to regret, relief.

Relief that she would get the distance she’d never been able to manage before. Relief that she would be safe from *this*. The tyranny of desiring what she couldn’t have.

Even though her brother loved her very much, she would always have had to make a union that mattered politically. Always. She could understand why he was opposed to this, but even if it wasn’t King Lucian, it would be another king here or there, a noble, a prince. Someone who could provide a beneficial alliance to Basilia.

“What are your thoughts on the matter, Andrei?” Onyx asked.

Of course he would ask Andrei. His adviser. The chief of his guard. His best friend.

Andrei shifted. “I don’t like it. She could be putting herself in danger. I will not allow that.”

“You are not in charge of me,” she said. “Your job is only to protect me in the situations that I put myself into.”

"Andrei will go with you," Onyx said.

"Excuse me?"

She couldn't imagine anything worse. She could not be followed into her new marriage, into the country by… She couldn't. The way that Andrei made her feel, the things that he aroused inside her…

Those were secrets that she kept locked down deep. For so many reasons they were impossible. They always had been. If her brother'd had any idea that she was lusting after the man sent to protect her, then he would no longer be her protector. He was like a brother to them, or rather he was supposed to be. The problem was, he had never quite felt that way to Emerald. At least not after she began to understand why men and women were different, and what made a man beautiful.

Andrei was beautiful.

He had black hair, deep olive skin and a perfectly sculpted face. The cheekbones and jawline of a model, but the ruthless intensity of a warrior. He was a puzzle. For no matter how long she knew him, she would never be able to get entirely down to the depths of him. He was a code that was impossible to crack. If somebody could have, it likely would've been her or Onyx. Given as long as they'd known him. But there were certain things he never spoke of, and emotions that he never showed.

He'd been sixteen, like Onyx, when the king and queen had died. Emerald had been twelve. She had been certain she'd seen tears glistening in his dark eyes that day, but he'd never spoken of it.

He'd never shown his emotion openly.

Even when he'd been a boy, lying in bed, just waking up to discover his parents were dead, his manner had been stoic. Grave.

It was his way.

But he hadn't left her alone in her grief. He'd held her while she wept, maintaining his own solid strength while she dissolved. Onyx had been the king, and while he'd been there for her as much as he could be, he'd been consumed with managing a whole nation rocked by the death of its monarchs.

Only Andrei had been able to concern himself singularly with her.

Theirs was a bond that defied words. And beneath that bond were feelings in her that defied what was possible.

"Of course I will," he said. "I will be a nonnegotiable addition to this envoy."

"But you live *here*," she said, panic rising inside her. "You can't uproot your entire life to follow me to another country."

"My service to the Crown is my life, Princess. Whether that service takes place here or in Alabria is of no consequence. You are my mission."

He was always doing things like that. Always undermining the emotional connection they felt they had with him. Always making it about duty and honor and his place. He wasn't royal, that much was true, but he was their friend. To her, he was a great deal more, whether he would ever know that or not.

Whether he would ever admit it or not.

You are my mission.

If he were any other man, it would be easy to take that as a declaration of some kind. But Andrei just meant that literally. She was a mission. A task for him to see to.

And he was ruining this. She needed to be away from him. She needed an ocean between them, a potentially psychotic husband between them. She didn't fear Lucian, because she'd gotten to the point where being near Andrei was the real source of her fear.

How long could she bend before she broke?

She was hoping to never test it.

"This is ridiculous. He's not going to make a political alliance with us and then *kill me*."

"I will assess the situation," Andrei said. "With your permission, Your Highness, I will send a missive to the Crown and let them know exactly what the princess will require as she evaluates whether or not she truly wishes to enter into this union."

"I've already agreed," Emerald said.

"And we shall add stipulations," Onyx said.

She threw her hands into the air, rage, desperation and her own throbbing heart making her lose control. "God spare me the interference of relentless alpha males."

She meant that in the most derogatory fashion possible.

Storming from the room didn't really help her case. She was trying not to be childish. But she had brokered the deal herself. It was a triumph of international relations. She was throwing herself on this altar, a sacrifice for the greater good of the country.

Well. That was exactly what Onyx was objecting to. But he didn't have the right. She wasn't weak. She knew that her duty was to the country. She knew where they were having difficulty, and she knew where she could make things better. Easier. King Lucian was the most difficult ruler spread across all the islands in this little belt of countries and principalities. She could tame him, then she could help everyone.

She remembered her mother, so beautiful and serene. She truly believed that her parents had loved each other, but she also knew that her mother had left a small village on the farthest end of the island that previously hadn't been joined together with the nation of Basilia. She had united the tribes there and the rest of the country. Had brought services to them. Had changed the lives of everyone for the better.

She wanted to be like her mother. She wanted to do something that mattered. Wanted to unite the nations. She had the opportunity to do that on an even grander scale.

It was her purpose.

What she knew about life was that it could be short and cruel. Even if she did meet her fate at the hands of King Lucian, she would've tried. Would've tried for a legacy that was bigger than herself.

The need to be her mother's daughter in this way was an almost desperate drive inside her. She'd lost her so long ago. This felt like finding a connection to her.

I'm the woman you would have raised me to be. If you had lived.

She heard heavy footsteps behind her, and she didn't

even have to turn to know who it was. Her brother walked on top of the floor. He was silent. Years of royal training had turned him into an elegant panther. Dangerous, certainly, to some, but smooth. Andrei did not bother to conceal his presence, ever. He was a blunt instrument. A weapon. And he wore that proudly.

"You are making a mistake," he said.

She turned around, trying to steel herself for the impact of him. Even though she had just been looking at him, she knew that he would make her heart beat faster now that they were alone. Now that he was closer. She turned, and she was right. Her heart leapt into her throat like it was trying to escape. "That's not for you to decide."

"Perhaps not, but I'm telling you all the same."

"I am a princess," she said. "And you are nothing. You would do well to remember that." She immediately regretted those words the moment they came out of her mouth. She didn't mean them. But she was angry. Angry at these men for undermining her. Angry at Andrei for making her feel things that were so at odds with what she knew she needed to do.

It was the worst of both worlds. Not only was her plan being hijacked by the most controlling men she knew, but she wasn't getting the reprieve from Andrei she desperately needed.

She didn't look at him again. She refused.

She was going to prepare herself for the sea voyage to Alabria. King Lucian did not allow flights in or out of the country, unless they were his own. Everyone, including the citizens of the country, had to travel elsewhere by boat if they wished to fly somewhere. It had always been rumored that it was a show of strength. A way that Lucian let everyone know that in his country he even owned the sky.

She didn't care what it was. She wondered if the ship's journey would deter Andrei.

That made her feel guilty too. But she didn't ask, and she didn't look back.

She had made her decision. Whether her brother and Andrei supported her or not didn't matter. She was selling herself into marriage.

It was a choice that only she could make. And she had made it.

"You could forbid her to go." Andrei was leaning against the doorframe, rage churning in his stomach.

Emerald was being a fool. Very unlike her. She was the most devoted, levelheaded person he knew apart from Onyx. This was a rare miscalculation on her part, but it was one.

King Lucian was a monster. The very idea of that man laying claim to her…

He could not bear it.

"Certainly, I could. And then what? Lock her in the dungeon? You have met my sister. She is the smartest person I know. Smarter than the two of us combined when it comes to matters of negotiation and the economy. The trouble is, it is a very good deal that she's brokered."

"Fuck the deal," Andrei said. "What does it matter? If her safety is compromised…"

"She is also right about the fact that it has never been confirmed he is responsible for the deaths of his previous wives."

"They're also all dead," Andrei growled. "So they can hardly testify."

Emerald was the most precious thing in his world. He would kill for her. Die for her. Whatever was required of him. His devotion to her was complete.

He had cared for her, looked after her from the time she was young. This family meant everything to him. When he'd been taken into the palace he'd seen love for the first time. Real love that wasn't filled with trip wires and toxicity. Unconditional, beautiful love like they wrote about in stories and songs.

He'd loved his parents, because he knew nothing else. He'd loved his parents because he didn't know children shouldn't see violence—passionate or otherwise. He didn't know a father shouldn't strike his son, or expose him to the dark, twisted dealings of a criminal empire. His father had often showered him with praise, and that had made up for the times when being in his father's sphere was hard.

His own concept of love, of family, was so perverted that he'd been completely undone by the purity of the royal family.

It had changed something inside him, and he'd sworn an oath in his own soul to protect this family with everything he was.

He and Onyx were blood brothers. After Onyx's parents had died, Andrei had cut his palm, and Onyx had cut his, and they had shaken hands, solidifying their connection to one another. Emerald was something else.

His.

And yet he knew that she wasn't. She never could be.

His desire for her was anathema to him. He did his best to shut it off, to push it down, to push her away. He'd been put in charge of her after the king and queen had died. He'd been made her personal guard—though he'd been young. After all, Onyx was king at that same young age, in charge of an entire country. Andrei had ruled over Emerald's safety. He had protected her physically, and had been there for her through her grief. She had become the person who mattered most to him in all the world. A connection that was not familial, but felt soul deep in a way he would never have been able to put to words.

Then it had changed. The intensity of the feelings had always been there, but then that intensity had become deadly. Like a knife resting flat on flesh for years, suddenly twisted so the sharp edge sunk in, deep and terrible.

The great and terrible hunger that had taken over him during a dance at her eighteenth birthday party. An innocent touch of her hand against his and he'd been undone. The fierce need to claim her, to make her his, to take her until they were both breathless…

It had dogged him now for six years, this deep caring that had turned into something so much more obsessing.

He exhausted his sexual energies elsewhere, faceless, nameless hookups that he found shameful in the broad light of day, especially when he looked at her.

But there was nothing that could be done. He was not angry now because she was marrying someone else. That had always been what was destined to be. He was angry because this man, this mad king, could put her in danger.

"This is why you need to stay with her. Obviously if you think there is any real danger to her safety, I expect you to put a stop to things. Start a war on your way out if you have to."

Andrei crossed his arms. "I'm listening."

"You will gather intel for me. You will tell me everything, about the king, about the country, about the palace. If we have to have an international incident, then we must. If you think that he will be unkind to her, abusive in some way, if you believe that it is a place she will not survive, then at any point during the marriage, you will remove her, bring her back."

"I promise."

"I know that I can count on you. I have trusted you with my sister, and her safety since she was fourteen years old. I continue to trust you now."

He smiled, but it was not a genuine smile. Because if he had any idea that Andrei's feelings for Emerald had begun to change years ago, when she had begun to look like a woman, and her sweetness, her care had gotten beneath his skin in a way that no one and nothing else ever had, he would likely have Andrei thrown in a dungeon for the rest of his life. Beheading would be too good for him.

"I'm sorry about the boat trip," Onyx said.

Andrei shrugged. Yes, he felt cold terror in his veins when he thought about going out on the water. When he thought about what it had been like when the ship had begun to take on the ocean, until it was more water than boat. The way that the pressure of the sinking vessel had pulled him down, and the way his lungs had burned as he had swum endlessly in the wrong direction. How he had washed up on the shore, he couldn't say. It was a miracle, he had decided. Because there was no other explanation. But every other man, woman and child on that boat had died. And so, he had always found it to be a sharp-edged miracle. Because if the divine had saved him, then surely the divine could've prevented the boat from capsizing in the first place.

He had a long-standing rift with God over that.

"It is nothing," he said.

Because when it came to the choice between his own comfort and protecting Emerald, he would choose her every time.

And so he would choose her now. Above all else.

If he had to lead her into this marriage that she had chosen, he would.

And if he had to cut her husband's throat to save her, he would do that too.

The one thing he would never do, was put his hands on her.

CHAPTER TWO

SHE DIDN'T EXPECT to get so emotional packing up to leave the palace. She didn't know what she had expected. But her resolve was so firm, she'd sort of thought that it would carry her out of the palace, onto the boat, across the sea.

Now, standing on the dock about ready to board the ship, she felt…frozen. Like her shoes were made of cement.

"Princess," Andrei said, "the boat awaits."

The boat in question was a yacht, beautiful and streamlined and with every modern amenity that a person could ever want or need. It was Onyx's, and Emerald had never spent a lot of time on it. She'd taken short trips before but never anything this long. Well, and never to her potential doom, or to a marriage with a stranger.

"I know," she said, looking up at Andrei. "Are you okay?"

He smiled, but it looked more like a sneer. "I'm doing just fine. Why do you ask?"

She immediately felt terrible, because she shouldn't

have even referenced the very real, and horrendous trauma he'd experienced as a child.

"No reason."

"Somehow, I thought as much." On wobbly legs, she began to walk up the gangway onto the boat. There was a staff member standing there with a tray of champagne waiting for them. "Oh, thank you," she said, taking the champagne and turning to look at Andrei. "Take one," she said.

"I do not follow orders," he responded. "Do I need to remind you?"

"That is strange, because you are here on my *brother's* order."

"I would be here no matter what Onyx advised. On that you can trust me."

He didn't take a glass of champagne, and she was certain that it was actually to antagonize her. At least it would be a comfortable crossing. All of her things had already been delivered to the plush cabin at the front of the yacht, where the views of the sea were glorious. The last time she had sailed on the ship Onyx had given her that room, and she had enjoyed it. But, she wouldn't go down there just yet. Instead, she opted to take her champagne to a lounge chair on the top deck and watch as they sailed away from Basilia.

She hadn't expected the grief. The tightening of her throat.

She was leaving all of this behind. This country where she had grown up, this jewel-bright treasure in the middle of the Mediterranean Sea. The only place that she had ever called home. The only place she had memories of her parents.

But she was doing it for her family. For her legacy. For her people. Onyx could come visit her, and surely she would be able to return home sometime. Surely.

She didn't have a chance to miss Andrei yet. Since it seemed that he was going to be her shadow this entire time.

Into her new life.

A ghost of everything she could never have.

She took an overly large swallow of champagne as the boat began to drift away from shore.

Conviction burned in her breast. She knew why she was doing this. She just had to hold on to that reasoning. To that conviction.

"Relaxing before your execution?"

She looked up at Andrei, dressed all in black, of course. "You are fun at parties," she said. "I know because I've seen you. Haunting the back walls like a wraith."

"Is this a party?" he asked.

"It could be. A beautiful yacht, gorgeous views, champagne. The only thing that's missing is other people."

"I never miss other people."

She laughed. "Of course not. Anyway, the more elaborate an event is, the more work goes into the security, I suppose."

"It is true."

She frowned. "What is my brother going to do without you?"

"I'm good at my job, Emerald. That means that anyone who has worked under me these past years is well trained in their position, and I leave behind competent people to coordinate the security of the palace. Only narcissists rule with such an iron fist that they cannot accept the assistance from those qualified around them."

"And you're not a narcissist," she said.

He wasn't. She was simply poking at him.

She did that with him, used humor, gentle and spiky depending on how exposed she felt, to make her footing feel sure with him. In return, he was dry. If you didn't know him, you'd miss that he was bantering back, because he did everything in the same, serious tone.

She knew him, though.

"No. I'm not. I am aware of my abilities, certainly. I am a realist. Not a narcissist."

He walked to the edge of the railing and grabbed hold of it, his knuckles white as he gripped it hard, looking out at the sea.

"I *am* sorry," she said. "About the sea voyage. I know that this isn't how you choose to travel, and it must be difficult."

There. She could be nice. She didn't need to bleed her desperation all over this situation. It would only make it worse. Complex feelings aside, and her irritation over all of the way this had played out ignored, Andrei was one of the people that she cared about most.

Bringing him with her should be a relief.

If she were normal about him, it could be.

"Nothing is difficult, Princess. I am more than able

to accomplish my tasks. What happened is in the past." And yet still, he clung to that railing. His eyes on the water, not on her.

"Where are you sleeping?"

"I have a cabin," he said. "Your brother was overly generous in appointing lodging."

"Let me guess. You wanted to sleep on the floor in the coldest part of the ship so as to adequately suffer for not being royalty, and my brother insisted on giving you a bed."

He lifted a brow. "How did you guess?"

He released his hold on the railing, turned to face her, a smile curving his lips. So rare were those smiles. His long black hair fell into his face, and the wind pushed it off his forehead again. His cheekbones were hollow, his jaw sharp, his lips a source of great fascination. Full and mobile, and having the appearance of a man who should know how to smile and laugh often. They kept him from looking as severe as he was.

They had riveted her from the time she was fifteen or so. When she had truly accepted that Andrei was something different to her than a protector or a brother or a friend.

That he was, in fact, the most beautiful man she had ever seen.

She felt so ashamed of it, at least then. Her palms would get sweaty, her heart beating faster, and there was simply no way for her to understand those feelings. Why for him? Why so strong? There were different points where she had come to accept what those feelings were because he was an unrelated male in proximity. The truth was, she had very little access to men unencumbered. None, in fact. Even when she had gone to university in the city, Andrei had been with her. It was always him. Always. Part of her had always loved that. Part of her had loathed it.

How was she ever supposed to be normal, have a date, have a kiss, have sex, if the man who consumed her fantasies, who was out of reach even though he was only an arm's length away, was always there.

How?

The truth was, she hadn't figured it out. And now the answer seemed to be: She had to arrange a marriage for herself.

So now her first time, her first kiss, her first experience of sex, was going to be with… King Lucian.

He was reclusive. There were no images of him taken in years. The rumors were that he was scarred. That half of his face was hideously scarred from battles during brutal wartimes in his country. The other half was beautiful. A fallen angel's visage. He was older. Forty to her twenty-four.

But that really wasn't her biggest concern. His age was simply a number when compared to his potential brutality.

Though all of these things were consistent across time. Men were brutal, and they wanted young women to help bear their heirs. She wasn't unique or special in the grand fabric of the world, and certainly not in the history of royal unions.

She wasn't marrying him for his temperament, nor was she marrying him for the joy of sex.

The joy of sex might have to be something confined to her fantasies.

She really didn't need to be thinking about the joy of sex while Andrei stood there looking at her with those dark, molten eyes, and that mouth that had bewitched her for so long.

"Is there any way I can dissuade you from doing this?"

She shook her head. "No. Why do you need to?"

He walked toward her, and much to her surprise, took a seat beside her in one of the loungers. "It has been my life's work to protect you. To keep you safe. I have followed you throughout your life. Every vacation you've ever been on, to university. And I will follow you here. I will guard you with my life, Princess, as I have done these past eight years. But it would be remiss of me not to ask you, to beg you, to reconsider."

"Andrei Ardelean? *Begging?* This is truly a momentous moment," she said, but her voice sounded breathless, and it was difficult for her to breathe.

He looked at her, his eyes black and hollow. "You are everything to me."

She was almost certain he hadn't spoken, that she had hallucinated his words, a trick on the wind.

At first she didn't react, because she didn't know how to. Didn't know if she should. But then she looked at him, her heart tripping over itself. He was staring at her with deep, focused intensity. He *had* said it.

But what did those words mean?

Was it *everything* as he was to her?

That seemed impossible.

"I trust you," she said. "I know you won't let anything happen to me."

"You didn't even want me to go with you."

She couldn't tell him. She couldn't tell him why she had wanted to leave him behind in Basilia. Why she was almost desperate to put distance between them. Did he have any idea how painful it was for her to go on and marry another man while he was right there. While she still had to see him. While she was still close enough to touch him, but never, ever could. Just like always.

Just like always.

"I *need* you to go with me," she said, finally, the closest thing to admitting she needed *him* that she would allow. "I see that now. Though, I do think you're going to have to look a little bit less suspicious of everyone and everything."

"I am there as your personal bodyguard. I don't think I need to look less suspicious at all."

"I do. Don't you think it would be better if they underestimated you. I mean, if there is going to be a problem."

"Perhaps. But if you're suggesting that I should play incompetent, I should warn you that I do not know how to do that."

"Incompetent at being incompetent? That sounds about right."

He made a short sound in the back of his throat and reclined in the chair. He crossed his arms over his broad chest, and she thought not to linger and notice every detail.

The strength in his shoulders, how his suit jacket pulled on his muscles. Andrei and her brother were addicted to the gym in the palace. They spent hours lifting weights and doing hideous amounts of push-ups and burpees.

They enjoyed pushing themselves to their limits.

Emerald did not.

Occasionally, she would watch a movie while walking on the treadmill. That was her version of fitness, and she was comfortable with it.

She often felt like Andrei and Onyx were attempting to sweat their demons out. Her demons took a different form. They didn't dog her physically. They were in her head, swirling around continually, day and night. Asking what her value was. Asking what she had done to make her life worthwhile.

At twenty-four, her mother had been a mother. She had been a queen. By thirty-one, she was dead. She wondered if all of that had felt like enough for her mother. All the things she'd done. By comparison, Emerald hadn't done very much.

"What do you see your legacy as, Andrei?"

He looked at her out of the corner of his eye, but otherwise didn't move. "My legacy?"

"Yes. Surely you feel like there's something you need to accomplish. Something you want to leave behind. We both experienced death at a very young age. I feel like it makes you think about it. And you experienced two times what I did. It makes me think. About what it is I'll leave behind, because the simple truth is we are only here for such a short time. Some of us much shorter than others, but there is no guarantee."

"My legacy, my hope, has always been in preserving your family. Keeping you safe. Keeping your brother safe."

"That's all? What is it that your parents wanted when they came to Basilia?"

"Safety," he said, his words hard. "They were on the run."

He'd never told her this before. The idea of him being a boy, running away from one danger and sinking in another…it burned.

"They saw Basilia as a potential safe haven," he said. "Though they never reached the shores, it was a safe haven for me. And because of that I fight to preserve the royal family."

"And because you like us," she said.

"Some days more than others," he said, his voice hard.

She was sure that he almost smiled. That the corner of his mouth moved upward just slightly. Just slightly.

"Today?"

"A trial."

"You don't ever plan on getting married? Having children?" It was a perverse question to ask, but she wanted to try and imagine his life without her in it. Wanted to make a picture in her mind of how things would be after she took this husband, after she left her home and him.

Any ghost of a smile disappeared. "No. My line ends with me. I know my father would have wanted me to carry on this line. Survival was paramount to him, as was the carrying on of his…legacy. He didn't succeed, except on one count. I feel sometimes that the sea was trying to take us all, but didn't quite manage. I have a mission, and that is to repay the kindness that your family showed to me, that your country showed to me. But that is all."

She frowned. "Why… What did your father do in Romania?"

He'd never said. Maybe she should have asked before, but she had a sense of Andrei, of certain closed doors in his soul, and she'd always felt like this was one of them. She'd assumed because of how traumatic the wreck and losing his parents had been.

But now she wondered how much more trauma there was in his past.

"There's no purpose to talking about the past. Especially, I don't wish to speak about my family right now." He looked around, and out at the ocean all around them.

"Of course. I'm sorry."

"No need to apologize. Though you are the reason I'm here."

"I know I—"

"I was teasing," he said, very nearly smiling. "I insisted on coming."

"It's a very dark thing to tease about."

"My life has been very dark so far."

She made a scoffing sound, and pushed herself up out of the lounger. "Will you join me for dinner, Andrei?"

He often refused to do that. He was very strange

about his protocols. There were times when he would agree to take a meal with her and with Onyx in the palace, but there were other times when he was hard-line about staying with staff.

His eyes met hers, and her breath caught.

You are everything to me.

“Yes. I will take dinner with you tonight.”

CHAPTER THREE

IT WAS A foolish thing to agree to. He should've insisted on maintaining his distance from her.

What he should never have done was tell her how much she meant to him. He wasn't entirely sure that she understood what he was saying.

That was for the best.

The cabin he'd been given for the journey was not going to work for him. He was never going to spend time in the lower decks of a yacht. Images of water pouring in from the top haunted him. He would much rather be on the top deck, where he could jump off into the ocean if he needed to escape. Of course, that presented the concern that if there actually was a problem he would have to find and save Emerald. And she had no issues with the ship whatsoever.

They were projected to have smooth sailing the entire way to Alabria, and additionally, the ship was sound and expensive, with many safety features that had been absent from the vessel that his family had stowed away on from Romania while on the run from very bad men.

His father had been a bad man, of course. And so

it was the exact sort of justice you earned when you yourself were a monster.

Still, the events of that day haunted him.

Which was how he found himself standing still on the top deck, looking out at the vast, endless expanse of water. It was a kind of blue he hadn't seen anywhere else. The surface rolled in a rhythmic motion, the surf so calm that the only whitecaps in the water came from the boat's wake. It was beautiful. But treacherous.

"Are you ready to eat?"

He turned, and his stomach went tight.

Beautiful. But treacherous.

Emerald was standing in front of him, her red hair free around her shoulders, curling delicately against her pale, bare skin. The dress that she was wearing clung to her generous curves, and the green, like her name, was a glorious foil for all her natural beauty. She had put on red lipstick, highlighting her mouth in a way that made his blood turn to liquid fire.

He was a man of great control. He had been alone with her countless times since that first spark had been ignited in his blood. He'd thought that he had mastered the art of self-denial.

But he feared, then and there, that that control had never *truly* been tested before. Out here in the ocean, surrounded by nothing but water, with Onyx far away on a distant shore, and his time with her running down like sand in an hourglass, his control felt much more tenuous than it ever had before.

Yes. He was ready to eat. But it was not food that he was hungry for. It was her.

If she knew the fantasies that he had about her, she would run away and hide. In spite of all the pain that she had endured, Emerald was an innocent. It was something that made him feel both pride and shame. She had never been able to date, had never been able to bring a man home, because he had always been there. Standing in the way. If he had been a different bodyguard, one who wasn't interested in her body, but only in the guarding, then perhaps he would've made space for her to have romantic entanglements.

As it was, he hadn't allowed it on his watch, and if he had ever observed a man showing interest in her, he had done his level best to scare the man away.

Emerald was untouched, and he knew it. Because no one had ever been given the chance to touch her.

Courtesy of Andrei.

"Andrei?"

He realized that he had lost himself, and the number of times that had happened was negligible. If it ever had before.

Normally, he was supremely in control of himself, and his reaction to her. It was always there, present, lurking beneath the surface like sharks out in the ocean. But he had dominion over it. Not here. Not now.

He couldn't afford it. He was going to have to be hypervigilant once they got to Alabria. King Lucian had the potential to be an enemy, a danger to Emerald, and Andrei had to keep her safe. Above all else.

"Yes," he said. "I'm ready."

"Oh good. I asked to have your favorite made."

"Why did you do that?"

"I don't know. To tell you the truth, I *was* mad at you and my brother."

He snorted. "I noticed."

"But I realized today how much I'm going to miss you both."

"I'm with you," he said. "You can't miss me."

He ignored the way that made him feel. He ignored his feelings with the same ease with which he drew breath.

With her though, it was always harder.

Suddenly her eyes filled with tears. "I know. But it isn't the same."

Why? Why wouldn't it be the same?

He knew why it wouldn't be for him, but suddenly he was desperate to know why that was true for her.

It was a question he couldn't ask. A question that he shouldn't even have.

He had never allowed himself to believe she felt what he did. But now…now he wondered. He shouldn't wonder. He shouldn't ask things like this.

So he shoved it down deep and followed her to where a table was set with white linens, overlooking the sea, almost as if it were a date, which was something neither of them had ever had.

Not with each other, not with anyone.

"Pasta," she said, smiling, making her way to the table and taking a seat that faced the water. He didn't need a view. He only needed to see her.

"I gathered, when you said it was my favorite." It was one of the first meals he had at the palace. A simple pasta dish with red sauce, and after everything he'd been through it had felt like salvation. It still did in many ways.

And she knew it. Of course she did. Because Emerald could never be accused of being a spoiled princess. Her actions, even now, were evidence of that. He might not agree, he might wish to kidnap her, take her far away from all of this, but he knew that what she was doing was for the greater good.

It was just that he didn't care much about the greater good. Not in the face of her safety.

He moved slowly to the table, taking his position across from her, and putting his napkin in his lap. He had a vague memory of when he had first come to the palace. Slightly feral, and uncertain of how exactly table manners worked.

His father never included children at dinners. Which would always have colleagues—people he had discovered later were from crime syndicates.

The kids had always eaten in the playroom. When he'd been young, he'd found aspects of his childhood to be truly wonderful. But he'd been in danger, and he'd never known it.

Not until they'd had to run away.

Not until it had been too late.

The king and queen and Basilia had taught him. How to be civilized. How to be less feral. At least in appearance. The truth was, his foundation would always be what it was. He would always be the son of a crime lord. He'd thought his childhood was fine, because he didn't know better. He did now. There were things his father had instilled in him, shown him, encouraged him to do, that had been twisted, wrong and vile. They were baked into him, part of the formation of his being. And he would always be a product of a childhood that had encouraged him to embrace his baser instincts.

He kept it on a leash with her. That leash felt dangerously close to breaking now.

"I remember the first time I saw you," she said. They never talked about this. The truth was, they were in each other's lives every day, and they didn't often discuss the past or memories. They had lived through many of them together. He had spent the first twelve years of his life in Romania, and after that he had been with the royal family. He had been with Emerald. The boat, the water, the fact that everything was about to change, that, he assumed was driving these conversations.

He wasn't sure what to make of that.

Or if he should indulge her.

But he decided to. Because there were other things he could not indulge, and so he would indulge in conversation.

"And what did you think?"

"I thought you were amazing. And quite possibly a merman."

That almost made him laugh. The sensation was so foreign, he didn't quite know what to do with it. "A merman?"

"Yes. You came right out of the sea. I know you don't remember when we found you. We were walking on the beach near the palace, and there you were, washed up on shore. Mother picked me up and tried to hide my eyes, because she thought you were dead. Onyx ran to you. Before my mother or father could stop him. He found that you were alive."

He had heard the story recounted to him before, but never by Emerald. He found himself fascinated. He wished that he had the memory, truly. Of that first moment when they found him. When he had been saved.

But it was lost to him.

"When they discovered that you were breathing, my father picked you up, and they began to run back to the palace. We had doctors there, and they immediately called for emergency equipment, more medical people to come and check you out."

"I remember waking up in bed," he said.

He wouldn't speak of the shipwreck itself. "Warm and safe. I was sure that I had died. That I was in heaven, though I did not expect heaven to have bedrooms."

"You didn't?"

"I thought you just sat on clouds."

Emerald and Onyx had been sitting on the foot of his bed when he woke up. Onyx looking grave, Emerald excited, her eyes shining brightly. "You're awake!" Hers had been the first voice that he'd heard in his new life.

"We brought you spaghetti, with marinara sauce and meatballs. And you ate it like you hadn't eaten for months."

"It's funny to me that you remember that."

"How could I forget?"

He refused to put weight to that. Refused to apply significance.

They ate their dinner as the sun set into the sea, and Andrei did his best to ignore her beauty, his reaction to it, how sore his chest felt.

He was not a man given to rumination. He knew his mission, he knew what he had to do. He had accepted a long time ago that there would be no love for him. No happy ending. No wife, no children. It was better that way. Better that he not continue with a poisonous bloodline. Better that he simply focus on serving Onyx and Emerald, being their protector, being everything that they needed him to be.

That was what he had chosen. It was the path that he walked. He couldn't deviate from it now that Emerald was getting married.

He had always known this day would come. He hadn't anticipated that he would have to watch it happen. That he would have to stand by and attend to her new life with her new husband. But he hadn't anticipated her selling herself to a man who might be dangerous.

"I know you think you don't want to meet anybody, but you might," she said.

"I won't," he said, his voice flat. He looked at her profile, graceful and elegant. The swoop of her nose, the curve of those red lips. He had met someone. She was the only person that he would ever meet who did this to him. He had read once about courtly love. About knights who devoted themselves to ladies and accepted the fact that it would never be physical. That it would never be anything other than honor and protection. That was how this would be. Always.

"We're going to go to Alabria, and who knows? The court might be filled with beautiful women."

"I will not be part of the court. You and your brother do not observe protocol the way that everyone else in the world does. A bodyguard, even if he is the head of security, is not part of the royal family. Nor will he ever be."

"I will insist that you are included."

"And I am not asking that of you."

"Well, I want you to be included. When there is a party, when our wedding celebration happens, I want you to be there as a guest."

"I will be guarding the proceedings to make sure it isn't a red wedding, so to speak."

"You are so grim."

"I'm paid to be grim. It is my job to be grim, and to be distrustful of the world."

"Will you at least dance with me at my wedding?"

He felt like he had been punched in the stomach. "You know full well a queen cannot dance with a commoner. Ever. Least of all at her own wedding."

"We danced before," she said softly.

He looked at her, their eyes meeting, holding. The impossibility of her request revealing in so many ways. Revealing things he'd never allowed him to see. A mirror of his own heart.

Yes. He remembered that ill-fated event. Far too clearly. He chose never to think about it. Chose to keep that firmly locked away in the deep, dark recesses of his memory. It had been a mistake. She had been just eighteen, and it had been her birthday party. She'd asked him to dance, and then she'd taken his hand in hers. She was so soft. Her fingers slim, her frame petite, and as he pulled her body against his he had felt desire like he'd never known before.

Need that went beyond the physical.

He wanted her. He wanted to cup her face in his hands and kiss her, but he wanted more than that. He wanted to be close to her, not just skin to skin, but something deeper.

Something he wasn't able to articulate or explain.

He could feel it echo inside him now.

"I don't think we will dance at your wedding."

"Then you should dance with me now," she said.

She was pushing. There was an edge to her now, and it was cutting deeply into him.

He wanted to tell her no. He wanted to scold her. Why? The only reason to do that would be… For the shameful, secret reasons that he kept buried inside himself. As far as she was concerned, the dance on her eighteenth birthday had been innocent. He was the only one who knew that it wasn't, and he would take that to his grave.

Why not? Why not take this one last chance to touch her? To hold her. Why not dance with her one last time?

He would not do it at her wedding. He would not do it when she was married to another man. He refused.

He stood up, and extended his hand to her. "All right, Princess, show me how you've improved these past years."

CHAPTER FOUR

She didn't know what she was doing, pushing him recklessly like this. She had been doing that ever since they boarded the ship. Trying to make him angry, trying to make him smile, trying to get some emotion out of him. Trying to see if he felt what she did. And now, pushing him into a dance… She was playing a dangerous game, except she didn't know if it was the kind of danger she was hoping to find herself in.

Andrei had never once demonstrated attraction toward her. He had never expressed interest in her body. Only in her protection. She was a duty to him, and she understood that. But she was also a woman, and he was a man. Of course, he had known her since she was a child, and it was possible that he would never truly see her as she was.

But now his hand was in hers, rough and big and warm, and he was drawing her toward his body, and she chose to forget everything but this. If this was the last time Andrei would ever hold her, then she would revel in it. Relish it. Then she would live and love only this moment for as long as she could.

She wrapped her arms around his neck, and he put

his on her lower back. There was no music; his gaze was intense.

You mean everything to me.

Those words flashed through her mind, and she felt electricity skitter down her spine. She was everything to him. Did that mean what she hoped it did? Did it mean that he wanted her?

There would never be another chance for this.

This was why she'd wanted to get away from him, so she didn't…so she didn't do this. But God, how was she supposed to deny it? How was she supposed to be given this time with him and do nothing with it?

She angled her face upward, bringing her mouth perilously close to his, and if it created any feelings inside him, he didn't show it.

Her own heart was beating so fast she thought she might pass out. His hands were hot against her lower back, and then he moved them, so that he was holding her hips. She couldn't stop the feminine sounds that caught in her throat, and she closed her eyes, willing herself to keep standing even though her knees had gone weak.

She opened her eyes again, and he was right there, all that molten heat directed at her. His expression was stern, and hard, and she knew looking for anything soft or welcoming in that face was a losing proposition. Except she could see the heat in his eyes.

He wanted her.

Andrei *did* want her.

A blessing, a curse. A total upending of everything

she'd allowed herself to believe. If she'd known he wanted her…

She would never have been able to resist touching him. Tempting him. Tempting them both. She couldn't resist now.

Not now, when they were sand in an hourglass.

"Andrei." She whispered his name, and reached up and touched his face.

He drew back as though she had slashed him with a knife. "Princess," he said. "I would advise you not to step outside protocol."

"There is no protocol for us. There never has been."

"Do you or do you not have a marriage arrangement with King Lucian?"

"I do, but…"

"But?"

"He is not on this boat."

"I see. And so you think a man like me, a peasant, should be happy to be your entertainment for the ride before you marry the man who is worthy of you?"

Her thoughts were racing. What he was saying wasn't fair, and it definitely wasn't true. She didn't have any experience. Wanting to touch him, wanting to kiss him, wanting… That was the momentous thing. It was not some throwaway, it was everything. He'd had lovers before, she knew that.

One time, when she'd been in a bar in university, and he had been in the back of it, brooding against the wall, there had been a woman who had sat down next to her and her college friends, and she had told the story of how the man in the back had taken her to bed and blown her mind, but then never called.

She was the one who apparently wasn't *special* enough for that.

Or common enough.

But she was too wounded to say that. Because what he'd said wasn't fair at all. She had never treated him that way. Not ever. She had never treated him as anything other than special. As anything other than one of the most important people in her life. And him trying to make this about snobbery, trying to make her marriage to Lucian about anything other than benefiting Basilia was utterly and completely unfair.

She'd been brave now. She'd been the first one to speak the truth of the thing that burned between them, and he'd humiliated her for it.

All while being a coward.

"If you don't want me, then just say so."

She turned, and left him standing there, and she didn't look back.

If he didn't want her?

He was plagued that night as he lay out on the lounger on the top deck, trying to sleep.

Of course he wanted her. He had wanted her all this time, and she dared to say that to him?

It didn't benefit either of them for her to know how much he wanted her. So he had not gone after her, and he had not sought to close any of the distance between them because that could only end in disaster.

It nearly had.

The way that she had looked at him, the way that she had touched him? God. He had been undone. All these years of practicing discipline. Of turning himself into a good guy. A man who could be trusted. A man who could not be called a villain, not the way that his father had been, and he was ready to destroy it all for her.

To burn the world down to touch her lips to his.

I would very cheerfully kill him.

Because there was no good end to it. There was nothing that could come of it.

She had run away from him, and it was for the best.

His phone lit up in the dark. There was Wi-Fi on the boat that allowed for messaging even out in the middle of the sea. It was Onyx.

How is everything?

As good as it can be.

Meaning?

Your sister is still marrying a man who might kill her, and I am taking her to her doom.

But everything is going according to plan.

According to plan. Yes, the plan where he sent Emerald to another man's bed.

Fuck.

He threw his phone down on the deck, and it made a loud clatter.

He heard a gasp. "What are you doing out here?"

"Sleeping," he responded, annoyed that yet again, it was Emerald. Yet again, he could not escape her.

"Don't you have a cabin?"

"Yes. I don't wish to make use of it."

"Why not?"

"Go to bed, Emerald."

She came into the dim light glowing from the deck above. She was dressed in pajamas now, her face scrubbed clean, and she was no less beautiful for it. Brave for standing there, facing him in spite of what he'd said. "I don't want to fight with you," she said.

"There may be no other option for us," he said.

"But why? We've always been important to each other, and everything is going to change. So why can't we be like we've always been to each other now."

"You do not always touch me," he said.

"No," she agreed, sounding subdued. "I don't have to do that again."

"I will need you to *not* do it again." His voice was hard, and he was aware of what he'd done here. That with this statement he'd exposed himself. His desire for her.

"Okay." She came and sat down in the chair next to his, her hands folded in her lap. "Look. I'm behaving myself." Her smile was almost impish, and it made the desire inside him rage.

He did his best to keep it on the inside, to not let it show. A memory rose to the surface, and he decided to speak it aloud. Anything to crush the desire that was threatening to stage an uprising inside him.

"I was on a lower deck when the ship began to sink

when I was a child. And I remember the water coming in from above. Beginning to fill up the room. If we hadn't been able to get to higher ground, we would've drowned then and there. I don't like the feeling of being trapped in small spaces, and I particularly don't like it when there is water all around. I am happy to sleep up here."

"Oh. I'm so… Sorry. I don't think we've ever talked about what you remember from that day."

"Because none of the memories are good."

"I know. But have you ever talked about it with anybody?"

"No. I remember everything about the shipwreck, until I passed out from not being able to breathe in the water. But I remember fighting with the water. I remember being certain that I was going to die, that the ocean was going to swallow me whole. I could hear the crew, my parents, other passengers, screaming before they went under." She had asked, and so he was telling her, though there was no purpose to any of it. To either being cold to her or kind to her, because none of it would change anything.

None of it would change what he had to be to her, what she was intent on doing.

"I'm so sorry. I would touch you, but I'm forbidden from doing that."

"Yes," he said, his voice rough. "You are."

"I think that if you weren't here I would be very scared," she said. "I think if I were doing this on my own… I would do it. I'm the one who signed the papers. I'm the one who made the agreement. I would do it. But you don't know how much you being here matters to me. To think that all those years ago I could have lost you in the bottom of the sea…"

"You have to have me to lose me, Emerald. And it isn't like that between us."

He was being cruel to be kind.

Perhaps he was just being cruel to protect himself. As deadly as it was to want her, the deeper, emotional need for her was almost worse. He needed her to not touch him.

It would shatter him. Everything that he was, everything that he had styled himself to be.

"I don't have you?" She squinted, looking at him as though she were trying to see him from a great distance. As though he were difficult to see clearly. "Yes, I do. You are with me all the time. Every day. You are my silent shadow, standing behind me, ready to put your life on the line for me."

"For the Crown."

"So, is it only my brother that you care about? Or is it the position. Your loyalty and allegiance to my parents, even in death."

"All of those things."

"But not me?"

"Not in the way that you are asking."

He stood, but so did she. "Andrei," she said. "I'm doing this for the country. Because this has always been my fate. There has never been another path for me. Just like Onyx."

"I know that," he said. "I know that. You must marry

royalty, you must marry for the good of the Crown. Just as I must not marry, also for the good of the Crown."

"And is that all we are?"

"Duty and honor? Yes. It is all we are. It is all we can be."

She looked ahead sightlessly at the black horizon. "I thought it would feel better. I thought it would feel like something triumphant."

"Does it not?"

She shook her head. "I wonder what my mother felt. When she came down from her village, the only place she ever knew, and married a man she had never seen before. I wish that I could ask her."

"That is one of the terrible things about loss. It echoes, continuously. There are always questions you want to ask, always things you want to tell them. But you can't."

They'd never spoken of such deep things. But everything felt different now, now that their time together would end. It felt like it all might as well be said.

She looked at him, her eyes glossy. "I don't know that I will ever feel like the fullest version of myself. Because somewhere out there perhaps there is a version of me who got to learn all of her mother's wisdom. But I didn't. All I can do is study about her in history books just the same as everyone else who lives in Basilia. All I can do is know her in writing."

"But you did know her," he said.

"I didn't know what to ask. Not then. I didn't know how to ask what I wish, so desperately, I knew now. I only ever asked her to do things for me. To read to me, to watch me dance. I wish I'd asked her how I should live. What makes a person brave? What made her brave?"

"I think that is the burden of growing older. You lose people, and realize all that you didn't say. When you were a child, your mother was only your mother. But now you see her as the queen. As a woman who made difficult decisions."

"Do you wish that you could ask your parents questions?"

"Yes," he said, standing up and moving away from her. "But I do not think that I would like any of the answers. You should go to sleep, Emerald. We have another full day and night of sailing yet."

"You say that like this is taxing." Perhaps it was only taxing for him.

"Either way, they are your last days of freedom."

He hadn't intended to say it. But he had, and neither of them could fully argue with the sentiment.

CHAPTER FIVE

These are your last days of freedom.

His words echoed inside her head all night. She couldn't sleep.

When she woke up, she felt wretched and grotty, and completely unable to control her emotions. It took a pot of coffee in a lovely silver service for her to even feel remotely civil. She didn't seek Andrei out until after that. She was sure that he had slept up on the deck, just as he said. She castigated herself for putting him in the position where he had to be on this journey.

She had been angry at him, and at her brother, but the closer she got to Alabria, the more grateful she was for the protection. The more she questioned herself, even if she wouldn't let Andrei know that she did.

Though their attraction—mutual!—was now out in the open, and it made everything feel electrified. It made breathing feel painful.

She didn't see him at the front of the boat, and wandered around the starboard side, taking in the view of the glorious Mediterranean before she went aft and stopped. Because there was an even more glorious view there.

Andrei. Swimming in the pool. He was shirtless, his dark skin glistening in the sun. He leveraged himself up out of the pool, the muscles on his body shifting with the motion, water droplets sliding down the hollows in his chest, his abs. He was wearing tight black swim shorts that did not cover his magnificent thighs.

He was a work of art. She had never painted a damn thing in her life, but suddenly she wanted to take it up. Or maybe sculpt him out of something. If it was the only way she would ever know what it was like to touch his body, she would take a hunk of clay right now and try to shape it into him.

Because at least then maybe she could caress the fine lines of his body. Wow, that was an incredibly weird thought. But she was in an incredibly strange state. The door on her self-imposed prison was about to close, and then Andrei would be out of her reach forever.

He's always been out of your reach.

Maybe.

"Good morning," he said, his dark eyes flickering over her dispassionately. She looked down at her loose pajamas, and felt annoyed. If she were in her underwear, he probably wouldn't be able to look so disinterested. It wasn't fair. He was basically naked.

"Good morning," she said.

"How did you sleep?"

She huffed a laugh. "Not well. Though I don't suppose that would surprise you."

"Because I don't like boats?"

"Because of my looming marriage," she said.

Manacles. Chains. A total loss of freedom.

How ridiculous to be so angry about something she had engineered. It wasn't like anyone was forcing her hand. Nothing other than her own desire to positively impact her country. Her own obsession with legacy.

But sometimes she did feel trapped by that. By her own impossibly high standards for herself and her life.

Now, see where it had led her.

He began to walk toward her, her stomach clenching tight, her… She could feel the echo of each and every footstep between her legs. Could feel herself getting sensitive, getting wet.

He was such a hazard. This wasn't the first time her body had gone completely rogue around him.

One time he had tried to show her some basic self-defense moves, and his hands on her body had given her fantasy fuel for weeks. She was absolutely sure that if he had any idea what she'd done to herself in her room after that he would be horrified.

Or maybe he wouldn't be. Because however he had reacted afterward, he did want her. At least, he had in the moment. But he was a man, so it could be that simple. He had a woman's body pressed against him, and maybe that was all it took. Maybe it wasn't about her at all, but just his sex drive.

He walked by her, his shoulder brushing against the side of her arm as he reached down and picked up a towel from one of the lounge chairs. He began to towel off his hair, his chest, and she found herself held captive by the motion. His chest, his washboard flat abs. His hip bones. Oh God, don't look there. Right at the center of those very tight swim trunks. The mysteries of the male form in all its glory were beneath those shorts, and she found herself very curious indeed.

Not that she'd never seen a naked man in pictures, but she hadn't actually seen one in the flesh. And anyway, he was the only one she wanted to see.

Lucky you. In a few weeks, you'll be seeing Lucian.

A stranger. A man she'd never even met. The idea was like a bucket of cold water poured over her head.

It wasn't that he was a stranger, if she was being honest. It was that he wasn't Andrei.

"What do you want?"

He sounded put out, his temper short.

"I don't know. I thought that I might seek the company of the person on this vessel that I know best?"

"You are staring," he said.

"You're a sight to behold," she said, not seeing the point in lying. He must know that he was beautiful.

"Stop," he said, his words short. Clipped.

"What?"

"You *know*."

He wasn't doing any better than she was. It made her feel strangely powerful. She'd felt alone in her need for him for so long. Discovering that he was tortured by it too? It was a heady drug.

"Maybe. But if you keep denying it then how will I really know?"

"I'm not playing games with you," he said. "Not for the entirety of this journey."

"Who said that I was playing a game?"

"You know how things are. A game is all it could ever be."

He turned and walked away from her, and she stood, mesmerized by the muscles in his broad back, immobilized by the pain in her heart.

The problem was her. She'd had to decide what she wanted. What she was going to do. This had been her decision, and she had regrets now. Maybe there was a way that she could have fewer regrets.

But he was right about one thing. She couldn't play games. She had to be certain.

He had been cruel to her earlier and he regretted it. But he needed his distance. What would she have done if he had grabbed her? Kissed her? Shown her exactly what he wanted to do with her. Shown her exactly how he wanted her.

She thought she wanted him, but what she wanted was a fantasy. She thought she could poke and provoke him as she might do some frat boy who approached her at university.

If she got a taste of his real need she would run, terrified, and she would have every right to. Because she didn't *really* know.

And instead, you'll let Lucian, the Sea Serpent of the Mediterranean, introduce her to pleasure?

The idea made him feel homicidal. And that wasn't beneficial for anyone. He had to be able to walk into that palace as her bodyguard, and not present as a threat to the ruler of the country, or he would find himself executed and quickly.

It was perhaps not a ringing endorsement for his mental state that the only thing that bothered him about that was the possibility that he wouldn't be there to protect her.

But in many ways, life for him would end after she married another.

Nothing has to change. She can still be yours in all the ways that matter. You will sacrifice yourself for her. Devote yourself to her.

Yes. That was true.

Without ever corrupting her, or violating Onyx's trust.

Yes. Lucian will get to violate her instead.

He growled furiously, angry, yet again, that he was trapped on this boat. If he didn't hate the ocean so damned much he might've thrown himself in to swim for a few laps. He was a good swimmer, and had become a better one in the years since the shipwreck. But he did not swim in the ocean recreationally. For obvious reasons.

It was growing dark, and they had made no plans to eat together. In fact, he had seen a staff member with a tray of food heading to the lower decks earlier, and he thought that perhaps she had taken dinner in her room. All for the best.

He walked around to the forward deck and saw Emerald, leaning against the railing, her red hair a curtain around her face. Her shoulders were shaking.

"What's the matter?"

She gasped, lifting her head and wiping her cheeks.

Then she looked at him, her eyes glittering with sadness, with fierce determination.

"I can't imagine."

"You don't have to go through with this." He would demand that the yacht turn around now and head straight back to Basilia. Hell, he would jump in and swim them both back. His fears about the ocean be damned.

"I *do*." Her stubbornness sounded nearly petulant.

"You can find another husband."

"Is that what you think? That this is about me being afraid of King Lucian? No. What I'm grappling with is that there's no way for me to marry someone who isn't you without feeling extraordinary pain."

He could say nothing to that. She had said it. She had spoken the invisible thing into existence. She had put into words something that they should never acknowledge. Something that he would never acknowledge, no matter how she changed the rules on them now.

"Emerald," he said. "You are emotional."

She threw herself at him then, as if she was leaping off a cliff, wrapped her arms around his neck and buried her head in the curve of his neck. The warm, soft press of her body against his undid him. He wrapped his arm around her waist, held her there, even though he knew that he should not. "Yes, I'm emotional," she said. "Because I'm never going to know. I'm never going to know what it could have been. I'm never going to know what passion is. Not really. I waited, all this time. I've never been kissed, I've never been touched, I've never—"

He kissed her. He could take it no more. He swallowed her words down like the sweet honey that they were, an elixir that turned his dark soul into sunshine as the sweetness of her mouth flooded him. He kissed her because he could do nothing else.

He kissed her, because he wanted her. Because he had wanted her all this time. She clung to him, her fingers pushed through his hair as she deepened the kiss, as she parted her lips and slid her tongue against his, as she arched her body against him, her breasts firm against his chest.

"Please," she whispered. "I didn't promise him a virgin bride. I don't want to go to his bed untouched. I want to have *you*. One night. Please."

He gripped her hips and growled. "No."

"Andrei—"

"Why should we light ourselves on fire only to burn? Don't you see, this is going to kill us both."

"I don't care," she said. "You're right. I was being frustrating before. Because I was trying to dance around the issue. I was trying to say it without saying it. Hot and cold, acting like your sister, acting like a jealous lover, acting like a spiteful ex. When the truth is I just want you, Andrei. With everything that I have, everything I am, I want you."

"You don't know what you want," he said. "You're far too innocent to know what you're asking for."

"You," she said. "Inside me. I want you to show me what passion is. I want you to show me what desire is. I want you to be the one to take my virginity. I don't want to give it to him. Shouldn't I give it to you? The man that I cared about for most of my life, the man who has protected me for all this time. It belongs to you."

But she could never belong to him, and that was the great and terrible truth. She could never be his, not truly.

But did it matter? Did it matter if she could be his for a moment. For a night. Would he take that and give her a lifetime of suffering?

He felt like he was standing on the edge of a cliff, balancing on the sharp edge of a sword. One wrong move and he would cut himself in half, but he was going to be cut in half anyway. She was going to marry another man. She was going to belong to someone else forever. That man would always have his hands on her. Would always have her body beneath his, because what man wouldn't?

So tonight, tonight she could belong to him. She could belong to him first.

Her kiss had been sweeter than anything he could've possibly imagined, and he wanted more. He wanted all of her.

He could have her.

And ever and always, all the days of her life, of her marriage, her skin would be branded with his hands. Always, she would have the memory of his cock surging inside her. Just thinking of that made his blood run hot. Molten like lava, his need for her as deadly and destructive as any natural disaster.

Nothing would make it better. Nothing. So he could suffer all of his life not knowing what it was to touch her, to taste her, to have her, or he could claim this. Just this once.

It was like drowning. Like dying. Like not knowing if he would ever reach the surface or if he was swimming to his death.

It was like his greatest fear, and his salvation rolled into one.

He growled, wrapped his arm around her neck, pushed his fingers through her hair and pulled her in for a rough kiss. He cupped her chin, holding her face tightly in his hand as he held her mouth open for him, tasting her long and deep, making her stand frozen like that as he gorged himself on her.

She was a revelation. A great and glorious beauty he couldn't get enough of.

He was so hungry for her he couldn't bear it.

His heart was hammering so hard he thought it might go completely through the front of his chest, leaving nothing but a bloody hole behind, and that would be a fitting tribute. For Emerald, he would give up his heart, his soul, his body.

He had already done so.

"We can't," she whispered. "Not out here. Not where someone could see."

He would do that too. Go down below, risk the entire ocean closing in upon them. As long as he was inside her it didn't matter. If they were his last moments on earth, then he would die happy.

He took her hand and led her down the stairs.

Let her lead him the short way to her cabin, her windows vast and open, facing the sea.

What a fitting way for this to end.

The ocean stretched before them. His greatest enemy. How perfect that it would be witness to this. He had gone down with a ship once before.

And now here he would again.

He sat down on the edge of the bed, looked at her. “Strip for me,” he said.

This would be her first time, and he would make sure that she was well acquainted with pleasure. He would make sure that this was the best sex she could ever possibly have in her life. No other man would ever be able to please her the way that he did because he had years of fantasies inside him. Years of thinking about her, and her alone. The curves of her body, the way that her face would look when it reached the peak of pleasure, the sounds that she would make. No one would have all that desire inside them for her, and no one would ever be able to make her feel the things that he did. He knew that for sure.

But as for this moment, the one where she unveiled that body to him, he would sit, and he would take that pleasure for his own.

She looked at him, her eyes never leaving his as she stripped off her top, a white, lacy bra underneath. Then she pushed her pants down her legs, kicked them to the side. Bridal white. Innocent white.

His.

She moved toward him, lifted her knee up and pressed it to the mattress next to his thigh. He lifted her up off the floor, bringing her close to him so that she was straddling him, his arm locked tightly around her waist.

Confession was supposed to be good for this, but the words burning in his chest didn't feel like they would be good for either of them. And still. Time felt like a loaded gun pressed to his head, and so he needed to speak. If not now, he never would.

They were doomed either way.

"You know how long I've wanted this?" he growled, looking up at her. There was confidence in her eyes, but also so much… Hope. It was the hope that hurt the worst.

"No," she whispered. "Tell me."

"Always," he said. "For so long. You have been mine from the moment I laid eyes on you, mine to protect. But then, that began to change. As you became a woman, I began to want you as a man. But I knew that I could never touch you. I knew that all I could ever do was protect you."

She shook her head. "Tonight I don't want you to protect me. I want you to corrupt me." She pressed her thumb against his lips, traced the outline of his mouth, and he closed his eyes, reveling in the sensation. "I want you to do unspeakable things to me. Things that you think might shock me, because I don't think they will. Do you know how long I've fantasized about you? You don't, do you? Oh, Andrei, I have wanted you. For so long. I have hated every woman you've ever taken to your bed. Even if I didn't see them, I knew that it was happening, and I hated them, as much as I envied them. There was a woman. I met her in a bar when I was in university, and she talked about how good you were. She talked about how you ate her. God, do you know how I fantasized about that?"

He tightened his hold on her. "It won't be like that between us."

"Why not?"

"Because I want you more. I don't know who that woman was. I wouldn't be able to remember her face if you tried to describe her to me. I never wanted her. I only wanted sex. But you… I want you. I'm starving for you. And I will remember this for the rest of my life."

She reached behind her back, unhooked her bra, let it fall free, revealing her pale, glorious breasts, her peach-colored nipples, tight with desire.

He had no control left in his body. He pressed his palm between her shoulder blades, brought her toward him, as he lowered his head to feast on her body. Her curves. He sucked one nipple deep into his mouth until she cried out, then he moved to the other, his thumb teasing the first one, using all the slickness he left behind to ease the friction.

She was grinding her hips against him, against his hardness, and it was all he could do not to free himself then and there. But if he did that, it would be over too quickly. And he wanted to savor this.

Because she was perfect. And tonight she was his. There would be nothing in the future. He would close that off ruthlessly at the bedroom door. The only thing there was, was this need between them.

This desperate, unending need that had built over a course of years. As far as the past went, those were the only memories he would allow. The memories of how much they desired each other. How much they wanted each other.

He began to unbutton his shirt, and she moved her hands, hastening the removal of his clothes. She pressed her palms against his chest, her expression one of awe. “You know how badly I wanted to do this earlier? I wanted to touch you so much.”

“Do it,” he said. “Touch me however you like. Taste me however you like.” They had all night. But it was only one night, and so it had to be everything. Every fantasy. They had to gorge themselves on it until they were sick with it. Because it was all they had, so it had to be everything.

She moved away from him, for just a moment, pushed her underwear down her hips and discarded it on the floor, naked and perfect in front of him. Her skin was pale, her curves generous, the red thatch of curls between her thighs the answer to his every prayer.

How long had he stared at all the beautiful copper curls on her head and wondered about the rest of her? For far too long.

He was seized by the same hunger that had claimed him before, and he grabbed her hips, bringing all her luscious glory toward his mouth, lifting her up off the floor and laying back on the bed, bringing her down over his face. She gasped, reaching forward and grabbing hold of the headboard as he parted her thighs ruthlessly and tasted all of her slick heat. “Andrei.”

“I will satisfy myself here,” he said against her. “And then, there will be more.”

He licked her, ate all of her sweetness, tasted her desire, his body so hard it hurt.

He moved his hands around to her glorious ass, holding her tightly against him as he ate even more deeply into her, as he felt her thighs begin to shake, as he felt her stomach contract sharply, as she cried out in sensual agony, as her release claimed her.

But he didn't give any quarter. He didn't stop. He kept going until she was shaking, sobbing, begging for relief. From the onslaught of pleasure that simply wouldn't end.

He was in pain, but he gave thanks for it. If he was going to die, then this was how he wanted to do it.

It was torture he would submit himself to for all of eternity. Pleasuring her while he was left in a state of arousal that wouldn't be satisfied.

It was his version of heaven and hell all at once.

"Please," she whimpered, but this wasn't just asking for him to stop. It was asking for more of him, and he could no longer resist.

He released his hold on her, and saw that he had left red fingerprints in her pale skin, on her thighs, her hips.

Had marked her perfectly.

She brushed her hair out of her face, damp with sweat, then she licked her lips as she moved forward, undoing his belt, the closure on his pants, and he was too far gone to make a game. He helped her strip the rest of his clothes off, helped her reveal his aching arousal, and when she leaned in and took his cock into her mouth he gripped her hair and surrendered.

She sucked him in deep, before releasing him, sliding her tongue down the length of his shaft, and taking him back in again.

She licked him like he was the finest of sweets, and he arched his hips up hard, forcing her to take him as deep as she could.

He could play this game forever, except his control was too tenuous, and he was afraid that he was going to come down her throat. Something he would've loved to do someday. With more time. With more hours to spare.

But that was for lovers who had the luxury of years. Of recreation. He had nothing beyond a few spare hours to claim her. And he would do it thoroughly.

Irrevocably.

He moved her head away from him, her face confused, dazed and pleasured.

"Mine," he growled, kissing her mouth as he laid her back onto the pillows, kissing her deep and long, pressing his body to hers, her breasts against his chest, her hips against his, the hard ridge of his arousal nestled against her slit. It was a moment that he was going to pause and be in. Her all against him, the scent of her, the taste of her on his tongue.

But then, he could savor no longer. He parted her thighs, guiding himself to the entrance of her body, testing her, and finding her willing but tight.

"Just a moment of pain," he whispered against her mouth before he thrust in deep.

The roar that clouded his vision, his brain, his body was primal.

His. Lucian might marry her, might claim her, might

have children with her, but she would never be his. Not in the way that she was Andrei's.

He would always be the first man to have her. It was all he could take. All he could call his own, and so he would.

He began to move, the feel of her slick, tight body all around him enough to make him lose control instantly. But he held on. This wouldn't be the only time tonight. He would have her until they were out of breath. Until their voices were hoarse from screaming out their pleasure, but there would be only one first time.

He wanted it to go on for as long as it could.

His thrusts were measured, slow, all in the interest of drawing it out. Of keeping them suspended in this moment, but then her nails dug into his shoulders, her back arched and she cried out his name. His name. "Andrei," she moaned. And he lost it. Completely. His thrusts became hard, totally uncontrolled, and he began chasing his own release, completely unable to put it off any longer.

And when he shouted out her name, it was both a curse and a prayer.

Because it didn't matter how many times he had her tonight. He was going to be haunted by Princess Emerald for the rest of his life.

And tomorrow he had to deliver her to another man.

CHAPTER SIX

When Emerald woke up the next morning, her body was sore. There was no place that hadn't been branded by Andrei. His hands, his mouth, his tongue.

She had been made his ten times over, in every way possible.

She was grateful for it.

But she wanted to weep.

She swallowed hard, looking over at the man sleeping next to her. He looked so much younger in sleep, carefree in a way that she had never seen him. He had been marked by trauma from the first moment that she'd met him.

And now they had scarred each other.

She might love him.

He hadn't said that he loved her. She blinked hard, trying to hold her tears back. She really didn't want him to say it.

Because if he's said it…

Better to let it just be sex. Better to let it just be one night. One night that she would never forget, but one night all the same.

She swallowed hard and stood up, and then there was a knock on the door that made her startle. “Yes?”

Andrei stirred, and sat up, the covers falling down to his waist, her attention completely captivated by his half-naked form.

“Princess,” came the voice from the other side of the door. “I have breakfast for you.”

“You can leave it,” she said. “I’ll only be a moment.”

He looked at her, his mouth a grim line. “I will go back to my quarters and ready myself to be presented at the palace. You should also ready yourself.”

There were not going to be any soft words for her. No goodbye. When he got out of her bed, he began to dress in silence. And when he left the room he didn’t kiss her goodbye.

She cried. For a few minutes, she cried. Because there was no way to fix this. Not ever. She’d made her decision. She had signed an agreement. She had given herself away.

But last night had been something she’d chosen for herself. She had to be okay with it. She was the one who had set the terms.

Still, she sobbed as she got dressed. Forgot that there was breakfast outside and nearly tripped over it when she opened the door, as the yacht moved into the port.

She wiped her face, but she knew that she looked like she’d been crying. Maybe King Lucian would like it. It was rumored that he was a ruthless bastard.

Maybe it would suit him.

When she looked out at the view of Alabria, she was shocked. It was a rocky, mountainous island, and a large black palace stood on top of the highest peak, like the tower of Barad-dûr in Middle-earth. All that was missing was the Eye of Sauron. If he wanted the world to think of him as a villain, he had certainly done a great job setting up the optics.

Dead wives not required.

She had been so focused on the grief that she felt over losing her chance with Andrei, that she hadn't fully allowed herself to feel grief over the situation she was putting herself in.

Because there's no point. Because you made your bed, and now you have to lie in it.

Hilarious, because the bed in her cabin still wasn't made. It was demolished from letting Andrei have her all night.

As soon as the yacht docked, they lowered the gangway, and as they were preparing to get off, they were boarded instead.

Andrei was immediately beside her, his hands on her as though he were ready to flee with her if necessary.

"We are emissaries of the king," said a man dressed in a military uniform.

"What makes you think this is a necessary display? This vessel belongs to King Onyx of Basilia. And it is very easy for us to take this as an act of aggression," Andrei said.

"Of course it is not an act of aggression," the man said. "A treaty is signed between Princess Emerald and the king. There is no aggression here."

Her heart hammered in fear as she allowed the group of emissaries to lead her off the ship and put her in a car. They paused in front of Andrei. "Your services are not required," the man said.

"I am the princess's personal bodyguard. I go with her wherever she goes. I think you will find the terms of that are nonnegotiable."

The man looked Andrei up and down. "I will leave that for the king to decide." He moved out of the way and allowed Andrei to get into the car next to her, and it was all she could do not to cling to him. She didn't have the right to do that, and he had made it very clear that physical touch, other than him protecting her, was not allowed this side of daylight. The car drove down a long, winding two-lane road that wound around the mountain, bringing them closer to the evil tower.

Reality was setting in very hard.

Warring with memories from last night. His hands on her skin. His body moving inside hers.

Stop this.

Stop this.

Stop this.

Her heart was beating a powerful rhythm, and the words echoing in her head were making it ache.

The car pulled up to the front of the palace, and they were ushered outside the vehicle. Andrei attached to her like a shadow at her back.

The doors to the palace opened, and they were brought inside, into a stark, black antechamber.

"The king awaits in the throne room."

A throne room? They didn't have anything half so prosaic. Onyx had a study where he conducted correspondence, and there was a sitting room where he entertained people. He didn't sit on an actual throne.

But it was clear to her that King Lucian really was stuck in the Dark Ages, just as the rumors said. The double doors to the throne room opened, and she stepped slowly inside, feeling like it was entirely possible that movement might release axes from the ceiling that were waiting to swing across the walkway and cut her to pieces.

She looked ahead and saw a figure sitting on a large, iron throne. Blond, his skin damaged on one side, perfect on the other, his eyes crystal blue, piercing through her from the great distance between them.

Whatever they'd said about his looks…they had underplayed it.

He was, in part, the most beautiful man she'd ever seen.

But where he was scarred, that beauty was ravaged.

"Princess Emerald," he said, his voice low, his accent indefinable. "Welcome to Alabria."

"Thank you," she said. "Your Highness."

She didn't genuflect because she felt that it would set a bad precedent.

"Let me see you."

He didn't move, he only sat there waiting for her to approach him. The way he looked at her made her feel like he was looking into her. "You are as beautiful as it is rumored."

"Thank you."

"You don't have to return the compliment," he said,

smiling, the scars on the right side of his face twisting garishly as he did. "I don't like lies."

She had nothing but lies to offer him, and it had nothing to do with his beauty. Because she might have signed this agreement, she might make vows to him, but she would never truly belong to him. She would always be Andrei's.

"You will spend the next month becoming familiar with the palace, our customs and my expectations. Then in four weeks' time, we will have a ball and a wedding. And our nations will be united."

"Of course your plan is best, Your Highness," she said.

She knew that it didn't seem honest. She could also tell that he didn't care.

She didn't know what to expect. She had thought that maybe he would want to spend some time together, but clearly he didn't. He waved his hand. "Show the princess to her room."

"And what about my bodyguard?"

He looked past her, at Andrei, as though he was seeing him for the first time. "The staff will find quarters for him."

"He has to be near to me."

He lifted an eyebrow. "Unusual."

"Is it unusual for royalty to travel with her own trusted protection to a country she's never been to before?"

"You demonstrate a lack of trust in me." He smiled, slowly. "Smart."

"A room. Near mine."

She could tell that it was costing Andrei to be silent. He was not her staff, he was so much more than that. He was a leader, through and through, and to be put in a position where another man held power like this was likely offensive to him.

But it would be foolish for him to behave any other way than he was now. Silent. Waiting. Deadly, she knew.

With very little provocation he would and could leap across the throne room and tear out Lucian's throat. That she knew for certain.

That was how she found herself bundled off to her room high up in a tower, with Andrei put in the one adjoining.

The temptation that she felt to open up the door between their rooms was real. But she knew that she couldn't do that. She knew that it wouldn't be met with welcome, not right now.

Because she was going to marry Lucian. She had made that decision, she had made that bargain, and for the good of her people, she couldn't turn back.

No matter how much she wanted to.

Marriage had never been about her feelings.

And it couldn't be now.

CHAPTER SEVEN

IT HAD BEEN four weeks since they had arrived in Albria. Andrei hated everything about the place, and he hated the king most of all.

He was mercurial, ruthless and odd. He didn't seem to respect anyone or anything but himself. Andrei also found it dishonoring of Emerald, in a strange way, that the man allowed them to stay in adjoining rooms. Not that either of them had used the door. He was standing in his control. He was here to protect her, to protect the Crown, the throne, and not to pleasure himself.

It was something that simply couldn't be done, and yet she haunted him at night when he tried to sleep.

His every waking moment was taken with his desire for her.

And he did not know how he might combat it.

It didn't matter. At this point, he wore it like a righteous mantle. Accepted it as part of who he was. The cost of protecting her.

He was being a martyr, and he knew it, but both he and Emerald occupied positions in life that demanded they martyr themselves.

What other choice was there?

Onyx was flying to Basilia with his wife, preparing for the marriage ceremony, and Andrei couldn't say that he was looking forward to seeing his friend face-to-face. But this meeting between the kings would be very important, one last chance for all of the diplomacy to fall apart, he figured.

There would be a rousing party in celebration of the wedding, and Andrei couldn't imagine what sort of party a king like Lucian might throw.

"Not a very fun one," the housekeeper said to him when he'd asked. This was the benefit of the way that he moved between worlds.

He could get information that other people could not.

"In what way?" he asked.

"Lucian likes to display his wealth and power. He doesn't especially like to share it."

"I see. And are the rumors about him true? Has he murdered his other wives?"

"Oh," the housekeeper said. "I think those rumors are greatly exaggerated."

"You *think*?"

"Yes. Lucian is coldhearted, that much is true. He is ruthless, but I don't believe that he's a killer, because it simply wouldn't benefit him. To kill someone implies passion. And I don't believe that he's ever felt passion for anyone, or anything but himself."

"You don't paint a kind picture of him."

"He doesn't paint a kind picture of himself. But then…" Her face softened. "I remember when he was a boy. Before there were troubles in the country. Before the attempted revolution. His own father was a monster, and then he was caught between a monster and a righteous horde bent on ridding this entire nation of a royal family that was corrupt. They tortured him."

Andrei nodded, not shocked at all. These were things that he knew from reading about the country. "Yes. And does he see it as his sworn duty to torture everyone else around him?"

"I think mostly he tortures himself. But again, I cannot imagine him raising a hand to kill anyone, much less a woman. Much less any of his wives, who were simply spoiled and selfish."

He thought the older woman was a bit overly taken with Lucian, but took her commentary to heart.

He carried the story with him to Onyx when Onyx and Circe arrived. "Your Highness," he said.

"Don't stand on ceremony with me," Onyx said. "It bothers me."

"Sorry. I have spent the past month engaging in nothing but protocol. This motherfucker has a throne room."

"Yes, I've been," Onyx said. "I cannot believe that my sister is intent on marrying him."

"She is."

He and Emerald hadn't even spoken privately in the past four weeks. He was there, doing his job, guarding her, as she got acquainted with the palace, and the people in it. He had watched her begin to relax there, had watched as she had found ways to make herself consequential, had found friends. It was wrong of him to find that enraging. That he found it irksome. He should be glad that she was finding her way in this life that she had chosen.

"It is good for the country, and I can't deny it, but I worry about her."

"There is no need to worry." Flashes of his night with her played in his mind. "You know I would die before anything happened to her."

Onyx got a strange look on his face. "Yes. I do know that."

Circe made herself absent during the conversation, as she always did. The tension between her and Onyx was always palpable.

It wasn't sexual tension.

She simply didn't like him.

Onyx could be a difficult bastard, nobody knew that better than Andrei, but he found his wife's dislike of him to be incomprehensible. He was a good man. He didn't deserve her vitriol. And yet he took it.

The night before the wedding was the event, and he could certainly see what the housekeeper meant. Lucian liked to show off his wealth. And it was on full display in the ballroom. The large, cavernous room was decorated with glittering lights, each one made from crystal—so it was rumored. There were twisted tree branches all lit up as well, the whole thing like a dark fairy forest. He wasn't simply demonstrating wealth, he was flaunting it.

The goblets were gilded, every plate studded with gemstones. It was ostentatious to a rather obvious degree, and it was clear that Lucian didn't care. He did what he wanted, and didn't care for the greater good, and yet he was marrying Emerald, which would benefit his country, and hers.

He was a strange man, and Andrei did not quite have the measure of him. It would be easy for him to call him bad and let that be done. In fact, that was what he wanted to do. Find him to be a threat so that he could cut off his head.

And yet it wasn't that simple.

The entire event was designed around Emerald making her debut, and he was positioned at the back of the room, waiting for her when she walked through the double doors and came to the edge of the steps, like Cinderella. But she was wrapped all in gold, as was everything else, and he wouldn't be surprised to learn that the dress was woven with real golden thread.

Her red hair was captured up off her shoulders in an elaborate design.

Her lips were red, tempting, beautiful.

He remembered that mouth being on his body. Knew exactly what those lips could do.

She would do that for him.

The burning hatred at the center of his chest was a living, breathing thing. His envy was a monster, and if it would not create an international incident that would utterly devastate both Emerald and Onyx, Andrei would've been tempted to kill Lucian then and there.

To carry her away like a marauder.

His father would never have allowed this wedding to continue.

His father had been selfish. He had cared only for his own desires. He would've picked a woman up and carried her off whether she wanted to be or not. He would've taken what he wanted, what was his.

He'd always known that about his father. It wasn't until he was older that he'd realized that was wrong.

He had decided that was a weakness. That true strength was giving desire over for the greater good.

He would do that now. Unless Emerald said otherwise.

He could feel a collective breath of the room catch as they saw her. Could feel the impact of her beauty, not just on him. She was ethereal, a creature from another world. Except he had held her body in his hands. Had touched her everywhere. Had experienced the glory of just how earthy she was.

It would haunt him for the rest of his life.

But he would rather be haunted by the memory than by what could've been.

He watched as she floated from person to person, a bee pollinating flowers, leaving sweetness wherever she went. He watched, and felt as if his heart was walking outside his body.

He had never loved anything in this world, anything but her.

The housekeeper was right. The party wasn't fun, but that could be because it felt like engaging in torture.

What a way to die.

He would give himself over to her protection now. To her mission. He would not compromise them, not ever again.

He repeated that mantra the entire evening. And when it finished, it was up to him to accompany Emerald out of the ballroom, down the hall and to her bedroom door.

"Good night, Princess," he said.

He turned away from her. "Andrei," she said.

He turned back to her. "Yes?"

"Is this how it's going to be? You… You're not going to speak to me anymore?"

"There is nothing to say."

"I think that you should leave."

Rage poured through his veins. It was like she had stabbed him through his chest with the sword. And yet he could see the wisdom of it. He shouldn't be here. He shouldn't look upon her every day, and yet he didn't trust anyone else to protect her. There could be no one else but him.

"You're a fool," he said.

"It's right. And you know it."

"Then I will speak to your brother after the wedding tomorrow."

"Good night."

"If it pleases Your Royal Highness. After all, next to you, I am nothing." With that, he bowed with no respect at all, and left her there, along with a piece of his soul.

CHAPTER EIGHT

She went into her room and closed the door firmly behind her. He went into his own, pacing, reaching. He wanted to tear the place apart, brick by brick. He wanted…

He wanted.

Tomorrow she would marry another man. Tomorrow, she would give her body to that prick. Without thinking, he jerked the door open that separated the rooms, the first time it had been opened since they had come here. She gasped, turning around, her hand on her heart.

"If I am to go, then I will leave you with a parting gift," he growled. He crossed the space and pulled her into his arms, kissing her savagely. There was nothing tender about it, it was none of the expression of tender feelings that had happened that night on the yacht. Where they had lived out so many fantasies in a short space of time, where he had devoted himself to the worship of her. No. This was about him claiming one more night. About him branding her one more time, so that she had to go to Lucian's bed with bruises from his hands on her hips.

It was cruel of him, and he knew it, but he would not allow it.

He would not allow her to go so easily. He would not let her be rid of him so easily.

He turned her away from him, so that she was facing the mirror, her back to him, and he began to lower the zipper on her dress slowly. Her breath hitched, her eyes closing. "Your body belongs to me," he said. "Don't you forget that."

Her dress fell away from her curves, and he leaned in and kissed her neck before putting his hand around her throat, tilting her face upward so that she had to look at them full in the mirror. "You belong to me."

She couldn't breathe. This was wrong. But then, all of it was wrong. Nothing was right, and it never could be, but surrendering to Andrei like this the night before her wedding was… It was a mistake. But she couldn't stop herself, any more than she could stop him. She looked in the mirror, at the two of them, at her face, which was like a stranger's. Her eyes were round, dark with need, fear, desire. She looked hungry, starving for him.

Such pointless honestly in a moment where it was too late. It made her want to rage. But all she could do was stand there, staring, looking at the picture they made in the mirror.

"Watch what I do to you," he said, commanding in her ear. "And you can think about it later when he touches you. You can watch yourself in the mirror as his hands move over your body. Watch and see if the pleasure is there, the need. It won't be. You will never want him the way that you want me."

"You're cursing us both," she whispered.

He was. Cursing her to a life that would never feel quite right. Cursing her to an existence that would always feel like half of what they had experienced together that night on the yacht.

She welcomed it, in a perverse way.

Wanted to sacrifice her sexual desire on the altar of Andrei and let it go up in flames. Wanted to punish herself for doing this to the both of them. For choosing to marry Lucian in the first place.

This was nothing like the first time they'd come together. There had been a joy mixed in with the bitterness. A sweetness.

There was none of that here. He was angry, and she couldn't blame him. She could do nothing but take it. Because she deserved it. She had done this. He tilted her head to the side, and bit her on the neck, then he released the strapless bra she was wearing, exposing her breasts, his dark hands cupping the pale globes before skimming down her stomach, beneath the fabric of her panties, as he roughly pushed his hands between her slick folds. She gasped, moaned as he began to tease her, torment her. She could feel the hard pressure of his arousal against her rear, the insistence of his desire.

"Watch," he commanded.

He pushed her panties down her hips, just above her knees, placed his fingers between her legs, spreading her lips open so that she could see her own slickness, the pink flesh there. Then he began to circle his finger around her clit before thrusting it deep inside her. Watching it felt obscene. And she was powerless to do anything but stare.

Was powerless to do anything but watch as he pushed a second finger inside her before dragging his fingers up toward her lips, and demanding that she open. "Taste yourself," he said.

She parted her lips and let him have entry, licking her own desire from him.

"Good girl," he said. "Would you ever do that for him?" She shook her head. "I hope you *do*. I hope it doesn't taste nearly as sweet."

Erotic confusion assaulted her, and she leaned back against him as he pushed his hand back between her legs, teasing her, toying with her. He had been a generous, wonderful lover their first time together, and there was certainly a physical generosity to the way he pleasured her now, but the emotional connection was gone. This was rage.

And it still felt so good.

He pressed his hands to the back of her neck and pushed her forward, then she could hear him undoing his belt buckle. He positioned himself at the entrance of her body, thrust inside her, and she watched the pleasure build on his face, watched it build on her own. The anguish.

And there was no small amount of anguish as he drove them both to the peak of pleasure. They made a profane work of art, there in the mirror, one hand on the back of her neck, the other on her hip as he thrust deep within her, driving them both to the limit.

Then he threw his head back and growled, pouring himself inside her, and she gasped out her own release, the waves of need rippling inside her endlessly.

When it was finished, she was covered in shame.

She'd given in to him, to his punishment because even that felt good. Even that felt better than not touching him. She'd been willing to accept his disdain, his hatred, on the eve of her wedding to another man, just as joyfully as she'd accepted their goodbye on the yacht.

Her going forward with this wedding had turned his feelings for her, she could see it. It had poisoned his love.

He hated her as much as he'd ever cared.

"Get out," she said.

"As you wish, Princess."

Out of her room. Out of her life.

Then he was gone. She wondered if he would even go to the wedding tomorrow.

Do you even want him there? What kind of sick person are you? There is nothing left for the two of you. Nothing.

She tried to sleep, but it was fitful. It was the night before her wedding, and it felt like a death march. But even more so when early in the morning she realized that for the first time in her life, she was late. And by the time the sun came up she had answered the question about why.

Thanks to the help of a sympathetic nursemaid, she acquired a test, and got her answer. She was pregnant, and it was not with her future husband's baby.

* * *

She knew what she had to do. Because King Lucian had said that he hated liars. And if she walked down that aisle carrying Andrei's baby then…

Maybe he'll set you free.

No. He wouldn't. He would kill her. And the baby. At least, if his reputation was to be believed.

Her heart was hammering hard when she entered the throne room. "I need to speak to the king in private."

"It is bad luck for the groom to see the bride on the wedding day," Lucian said. "And you should believe that, because my brides have had very bad luck."

"I will risk it."

He waved his hand and the guards melted away.

"And where is your ominous shadow?"

"I assure you, I don't know."

"I see. And what is it you have to tell me?"

"I'm pregnant."

"I have been told my virility is powerful, but I believe this is pushing the limits even for me," he said.

"Obviously it isn't yours."

He shrugged. "That is of no matter to me. It speeds along the production of an heir, but don't think that it will spare you the wedding night."

"You don't… You don't care?"

"No. I've lost two wives without the benefit of an heir. This is a boon for me."

"But most men—"

"Blood means nothing to me," he said. "You mean nothing to me. I don't care if you fuck your brother's entire guard, or just the one. Am I clear?"

She clenched her teeth together. "You have no interest in calling the wedding off?"

"None. And in fact if you were to do so, the consequences would be disastrous. For you. I would find them enjoyable."

"Then I will see you in a few hours."

The reality of the situation was about to crush her. Her wedding gown was beautiful, but it was for a woman with an entirely different sense of style. Lucian had chosen it, because this was his play, and she was merely one of the players. She was a pawn. Just like her baby was.

Hers and Andrei's baby.

But Andrei was gone, and she had no choice.

She was on the verge of panic. She couldn't think clearly. She felt like she was halfway down death's road, her whole body strung tightly with anxiety and fear. Going forward with the marriage felt impossible. Leaving felt fatal. So all she could do was go through the motions. Go along with the plan already in place.

Before she knew it, it was time for her to walk down the aisle. Onyx took her arm and looked at her, a strange sort of sadness on his face.

"What?"

"I don't know. Something about it doesn't feel right."

"It's too late. I've signed the agreement."

"I support you, Emerald, and whatever it is you need."

She nodded, and she and her brother began to walk down the aisle. At the head of the aisle was Lucian, and behind him a priest, kneeling in prayer, his back turned.

He was wearing blue robes, with a large cross on the back. A symbol of torture and salvation, depending on the context. Right now, it felt like torture.

Stop this.

Stop this.

Stop this.

But she didn't. She couldn't. For the safety of the country. For the safety of her baby.

Her legacy didn't feel like it mattered much anymore.

When she arrived at the head of the aisle, Onyx released his hold on her, and Lucian extended his hand. She took it, and found herself standing across from him at the altar.

The priest rose slowly, and then he turned.

And her heart dropped into her feet. "Andrei?"

"Oh. The guard," Lucian said, looking at him and then out at the crowd. "This is a bit dramatic."

"It is," Andrei said. "Because I wanted you to know. I wanted everyone here to know, who it is who took your woman. Surprise. She's mine now."

He wrapped his arm around her waist, lifted her up and brought her up against his chest. "I'm taking her somewhere you won't find her."

"Guards," Lucian shouted.

But Andrei was too quick. He had a plan.

There was a clear route, diagonally and through the back door, and then they disappeared suddenly into a side passage that spit them out outside. And somehow, no one followed them that way. "What are you doing?"

"You didn't think that I was going to let you marry him? I'm only shocked that you let yourself get that far."

She looked at his face, and she saw that something was irrevocably broken between them.

Whatever feelings he had for her before, they weren't there now. He was being driven by fury. Possessiveness.

Rage.

He must've found out about the baby.

But she didn't have time to ask him, because suddenly, she was being gathered more tightly against him, and he jumped off the edge of a cliff, taking them both down into the churning sea.

CHAPTER NINE

THEY WERE DROWNING. Together. He didn't know which way was up. He didn't particularly care. For a moment, he just let it all not… Hurt.

And then, his body sprung into action.

He began to swim them both toward the surface of the water. Up and up, to where he had the small boat moored against the side of the rock.

He had given up all his honor for this. For them. He had gone to the darkest place inside him to claim her as his. This might be sharp, hard, she might be angry that he'd thwarted her, but he could not allow her to give herself to another man.

He'd thought he could.

But he was his father's son.

He'd run from that all his life, until he'd needed to run to it. And now he was embracing it. Along with his fury. She should have felt the same way. She shouldn't have been able to go through with it—as he hadn't been able to allow it.

She hadn't, and he was angry about that.

But he had her now. And no matter how angry he was now, he wouldn't let her go.

Not ever.

He hauled them both into the boat, starting up the motor and moving them away from the coastline as quickly as possible.

"Are you *insane*?" she sputtered, her white dress in tatters, her hair a wreck.

"Yes," he said.

"You could've killed us both."

"But I didn't."

"You could have. You could have… And the baby."

He froze. "The baby?"

"That's why you came for me, isn't it?"

"What baby, Emerald?"

She was waxen already, utterly pale, but all the remaining color flooded away from her face as she stared at him. "You didn't know?"

"No. I didn't fucking know. I still don't. Tell me. Now."

"I… Andrei, I'm pregnant."

Rage. Rage and this crushing, relentless pain in his chest was all he knew.

She was pregnant with his baby, and she had been planning on marrying Lucian? Had been planning to give not just herself, but his child to another man.

It changed everything.

This had been about them. He'd been wounded that she'd been able to let it go so far, that she had kept walking toward this inevitability while he had broken.

In the stillness of the night, the ghost of his father had visited him. In the form of his own disgust. And it demanded to know why any son of the Ardelean crime family would behave with such cowardice. Would put the greater good over what he wanted. Needed. Deserved.

But now things had taken an even darker turn. Her willingness to marry another, and now the realization that she'd been trying to pass his child off as another man's, made a mockery of them. Everything they were. Everything they had ever been.

He had been the one to go back on his word by taking her, by not allowing her to do what she felt was right, was her duty. And he had felt weak for that. But knowing now that she was pregnant with his child, knowing now that she had intended to pass that child off as belonging to another man, all of his illusions, and his guilt, shattered.

"I signed an agreement."

"When did you find out?" The salt air was in his face, the spray of the sea lapping up against the boat, and it was not fear he felt now. Rage.

"I..." Her teeth were chattering, and had he been in a different mood, had it been a different moment in time, he would have done everything he could to keep her warm.

But everything had changed in the space of a breath. From the time they had gone beneath the surface, to when they had come up. Nothing was the same, and it never would be again.

"Did you even go to bed with me, say goodbye to me, knowing that you were pregnant with my child, withholding this information from me?"

"No," she protested. "Andrei, of course I didn't know.

I found out this morning. I realized that I never had my… I realized that I was late. Ever since the yacht, and I hadn't thought about it because everything has been mixed up since that day. I didn't know. I had very little time to figure out what I was going to do. You were gone."

"I would have answered your call."

"I know that. But I thought that when I told Lucian…"

"He knows?"

"Yes. I told him."

"And he decided to steal my child?"

She nodded. "He needs an heir. He said that it didn't matter to him because… He's been married twice, and neither of his wives has lived long enough to produce heirs. He thought that it was convenient that I was pregnant already."

"Then he is a monster. But so are you."

She said nothing more. Her unwillingness to fight him, her lack of desire to explain herself, spoke volumes. There was no sound, only the motor of the boat, the crash of the waves. They weren't being pursued. It would be a very slow trek to the island of Marake, where he had arranged air transport for them. They had three hours in this boat, and frankly, if Lucian realized that they had taken to the sea, he would be able to overtake them in just about any air- or watercraft he chose.

Andrei had to continue to hope that it didn't occur to him.

And that if Onyx were to give any guidance, even

genuine guidance, he would say that Andrei would never take to the sea.

But he didn't know. He did not know the ferocity of his feelings for Emerald, nor the things that had happened on the water in these past weeks.

The way that it had changed him.

"Where are we going?" Her teeth were chattering; she had been silent for what felt like an hour.

"Somewhere warmer than this."

The journey on the water was brutal. Emerald's stomach was churning by the time they got off the boat, and she found herself bundled onto a private jet.

"How do you have… Access to this?"

Andrei turned to her, his expression severe. "You think I do not have money of my own? Do you think I have not taken what your brother has paid me and made investments? You truly do think me common."

"I don't, I…"

She was miserable. She should be ecstatic. Andrei had come for her. She was pregnant with his baby. But this was like being on the other side of the looking glass. As if she had stood there, seen her dream and fallen down into the other side, been presented with a backward, twisted version of the thing that she had always wanted.

Because she had hurt him. She could see it. He was furious in a cold, frightening way. She wasn't sure that they would ever recover from it.

The truth was, what she'd done had been a decision made in shock. Likely, she would've come to her senses at some point, but everything would've been more complicated. It was a narrow escape, this brush with marriage to the wrong man, but now she had fallen out of the frying pan and into the churning waves.

"I really didn't have time to think—"

"I was going to take you. Regardless. I had no idea about the child."

He sat down in a plush, leather chair, forearms rested on the arms, his legs spread wide. He was wet, and furious. She stood, unwilling to sit down, unable to. Her whole body was trembling.

"If you do not sit when we prepare for takeoff, you will fall over."

She did sit then.

"I could not give you to him. But I had no idea what a treacherous woman you were. Still, all the better that I did take you, or I would have been denied my child. I have lost all of my family, Emerald, and you would take my child from me too."

"I didn't think of that. I didn't… I didn't think."

"No," he said. "You didn't think of anyone but yourself. Your legacy, is that not correct? That is all you think of. The way that you will be written about in the history books. Well, I don't know about the history books, but what happens today will surely be written about in headlines the world over. And our child will be able to read those headlines. What do you think they will make of them?"

She wasn't sure that it mattered, because she didn't know she was going to survive this. She didn't know if she was going to survive any of this. It also wasn't true.

"It isn't about what they write about me. I wanted to do the right thing," she said.

"How could right have ever been *this*?"

She had no idea. But every moment since this morning had been the shortest and longest of her life. She was tongue-tied. She hadn't said half of what she should have said—to him or to Lucian.

Now she had been kidnapped by a man who hated her, she was pregnant with his baby, everything felt like it was imploding and Lucian might start a war. Lucian. "You know there's going to be consequences for Basilia."

"Yes," he bit out. "I do know that. But I have kept your brother out of this. He knows nothing, nor does he know where we're going."

"He's going to find us."

"He won't. We are going to disappear."

"You seem so confident in that."

"I am. I am the head of security for a major nation. Do you think that I don't know how to hide? You think that I do not understand what is at stake? Do you think I did not calculate these risks? Pity that there was one major factor I wasn't aware of. Your faithlessness."

She sat down in the chair, shivered. "That isn't fair. I told you what I would be faithful to. I told you what I was going to do, and why it was essential for me to do it. You knew. You knew what was important to me. You knew that I was fixed on this, that I was doing this for Basilia."

"Everything changed."

But why had he only taken her now? Why hadn't he offered her anything before?

She wanted to cry. Because he was right. Everything had changed. Not just when she had discovered she was pregnant, but from the moment they touched. And now she had fractured them. She was not her mother. She wasn't brave. She made the wrong choice, and she didn't know how they could recover from it.

"Are you going to tell me exactly where this plane is taking us?"

"No," he said.

She didn't have her phone, anyway, to message anyone. And also, there was no way for her to be tracked. She imagined that was a handy side effect of her being kidnapped straight from the altar. How nice for him.

"You should go and get changed," he said.

"I'm fine."

"You are not fine. You're going to catch your death." She was in a wet wedding dress. It really was quite ridiculous. The fabric was ruined, sodden. Just like everything else.

"I don't have anything with me."

"Foolish woman. You think that I took you without making preparation for you? Do you think that I planned to fling you into the sea without providing you with warm clothes?"

He got up and went to the sideboard, took out a bottle of whiskey and poured himself some. "You cannot have any. Therefore, you will have to warm yourself by getting dressed."

She stood, her hands trembling. "All right. I will."

She tried to keep her head held high, tried to hang on to some semblance of pride. She didn't like that he was giving orders and that she was obeying them, but this was an order that she really quite wanted to obey. All things considered. She was freezing. She went into the bedroom at the back of the plane, and opened a closet in there. Turbulence rocked her and the hangers just slightly, and she cursed that she tripped over the wet, sodden dress.

Then she dug through all the clothes, found a pair of sweats and elected to go with those. She had no one and nothing to impress after all.

It was such a funny thing. She had treasured, obsessed over, and loved Andrei for so many years. And yet he had seen her in sweats, pajamas and now nothing. He knew her better than anyone. And now he hated her.

It was an extremely brutal reality that she found herself living in.

She stripped the dress off, her skin clammy, and tossed it into the bathroom that was next to the bedroom. Then she slipped on the sweatpants, the sweatshirt.

And as she was doing so, she had the full realization of what had happened today.

Of what Andrei had done. He had jumped off a cliff into the water with the two of them. He had taken her across the ocean to another island.

He was afraid of the water, even if he would never have said it that way. But he had violated his own rules about the sea, had taken her in the cabin downstairs so that he could be with her, and then had engineered this rescue that should've gone against everything he'd designed his life around.

The rescue itself violated his life's work. And he had done it anyway.

It made her feel sick with guilt. Regret.

But then… He would've kidnapped her today even if she weren't pregnant. He didn't know about the baby.

She didn't know whether that made her feel a strange sense of joy, or rage. He hadn't put the country first. He hadn't…

He had put her first.

Or just him.

But knowing that he wanted her that much was a strange sort of intoxicating elixir she had never known had the potential to be quite so powerful.

She came out of the bedroom, and he was getting dressed. He was wearing only a pair of black pants, and just as she came out, he pulled a white T-shirt on over his muscles.

How could he be so familiar to her, but so novel all at the same time? How could he be the man that she had known for most of her life, and also a stranger? The object of her fantasies, but also a fantasy fulfilled, and one pushed even farther out of reach.

She knew him well enough to know that his fury was not something to take lightly. Knew him well enough to know that this was not a small slight in his eyes.

He would make her pay for this. Possibly for years to come. He had made it so that Onyx couldn't save her, and while she knew that for Andrei, protecting her was paramount, she also knew that she was his now.

Whatever that meant.

"We both had the same idea," she said, trying to force a smile.

"Don't," he said. "Don't speak to me like nothing has changed."

"I made the decision that I made," she said. "It was the only one that I could think to make at the time. But you planned to undermine my decision all along. So I'm not certain that you have the right to be quite this angry at me."

"You would deny me my child."

The words were like a knife. He was singular in his feeling on that, and he wasn't going to shift. She couldn't blame him. The truth was, staring at that through his dark, outraged eyes, she saw the flaw in her decision. Immediately. She couldn't justify it. But she wanted to. She wanted him to believe the best of her, even now. It was such a strange, hollow sensation, this need to cling to the choice she'd made while also feeling that her choice had been a cowardly one.

One that she would've regretted. One she regretted now.

"We will land soon," he said. "We're not going far away."

"But how do you expect we're going to hide?"

"Because we're going back to Romania. To my father's house."

"Your father's house? Don't you think that it's certain that we'll be found in that case?"

"No. Nobody knew about the estate. The whereabouts of the property of the Ardelean Crime Family are very secretive. My father told me this when I was a boy. Then I have known ever since."

"You… Crime family?"

"Yes. My father was fleeing persecution of his own making, Princess. My father was not a good man. But, that has its uses for me now. I wanted to be different than him. I didn't wish to treat a woman like a position. I did not wish to put the needs of myself above the needs of a nation. And yet, now I find that I feel differently. Because your wishes have no place here. And nothing matters but that I get what I want. And what I want is you. I would have taken you to be my wife. But now I'm happy to keep you as a prisoner. You are used to seeing me in your brother's kingdom. But in my home, no other man sits on the throne. There, I am your king."

CHAPTER TEN

THE WATER WAS so blue.

She didn't know what she had expected Romania to look like, but in truth, she had imagined something dreary and grim.

A sort of Soviet blockade.

But this was all green mountains wreathed in mist, and the unfiltered light of the sun. It was glorious. But she didn't want to say that. The plane landed at a small airport, and from there they were put in a helicopter, which carried them high over the mountains until they arrived at the top of one, and there, nestled in trees was what could only be described as a fortress. It was made from natural gray stone, blending in with its surroundings. Vines and roses climbed all over the walls, as though nature was trying to draw it back into itself.

She wondered how many years it had been since anyone had occupied this place.

"I had it prepared for you," he said. "I hired people from down in the village to come and make sure that it was ready for habitation."

Since he seemed to be reading her thoughts, his words going directly into her ears, the headphones she wore for the helicopter ride making that possible, she decided she might as well ask the question.

"How long has it been since anyone lived here?"

"Since we left for Basilia. Under cover of darkness. We did not take a helicopter. We hiked through the mountains. Swam through the rivers. Until we arrived at the sea."

"Oh."

She found herself feeling sympathy for him, even as she had been proclaimed his prisoner.

Perverse, perhaps.

Well, definitely.

The helicopter began to descend, and she found herself looking for something to hold on to. The most logical thing would have been Andrei, but she did not want to touch him now.

It seemed wrong.

The helicopter landed in a barren field, and she and Andrei got off. Nobody got off with them. And once the helicopter lifted back up in the sky, the wind howling around them, they were the only ones there, shrouded in the wilderness, enveloped by trees. She could still hear the helicopter rotors in the distance, but otherwise, it was all birds.

He was looking around, marveling at the place with just as much interest as she was.

"Have you been back here at all?"

"No. I was pleased to discover that it was still standing, though the condition will be an interesting thing to discover. I was sent photographs, but I had to act quickly. Now you see why I say you will not be found."

"And you think that we can just stay here forever?"

"I think that we will stay here until I say otherwise. Don't worry, I will contact Onyx."

"I want to talk to him."

"Not now."

She felt a sort of hollow, cascading terror. This was nothing she had ever expected. This was a side of Andrei that she had never seen. But he was right. She had always seen him in a country that wasn't his own. She had always seen him next to her brother, to whom he had sworn a level of allegiance and loyalty. But obviously there was a breaking point to that. She had found the breaking point.

He began to walk ahead of her, through the dense trees. And she hurried quickly after him. Whether she felt any symptoms from her pregnancy or not was difficult to say. She felt nauseous, that much was certain. But there were a lot of reasons for her to feel nausea right now.

The trail was overgrown, and even though he hadn't been back here since he was a child, she was beginning to suspect that he might not know exactly where they were going. Until they came to an overgrown gate.

He looked up, and she was certain that there must be security cameras. "Andrei Ardelean is here to take his rightful place."

The gates opened, and he went inside. He didn't touch her. Of course he didn't. Of course he didn't.

She went after him and into the garden. It was like an enchanted space. It wasn't only the walls that were overgrown. Here, ivy had taken over everything. It was glorious and wild. Utterly unexpected.

But then, none of this was expected.

They walked through the shaggy hedges, the untamed greenery, until they came to a small door. Not the main entrance of the house. It opened for them without him having to knock.

And there was a small woman standing there, her white hair captured in a bun. “Andrei,” she said. “I knew you would return home one day.”

His face shifted, shock on his features. “Rebecca?”

“Of course. We kept this place for you. We knew that you were alive. Word of your survival made it back here.”

“And why did Ricardo never come for me?”

“With your father dead, there was no point going after you. Particularly not when you were protected by the royal family and Basilia. I heard, as well, that the king there paid him in political favors to leave you alone.”

Her father had kept Andrei safe. All this time. Even in death. Emerald was shocked.

“I did not expect to find you here,” he said, his voice rough.

“I have nowhere else to go.”

“Weren’t you all at risk?”

She shook her head. “Your father’s death released us all. This place always remained secret outside the scope of the village. He was afraid that would change. But it didn’t.”

“We could’ve simply stayed here.”

She shook her head. "No. You would've been trapped here for all your days. Your father never could've lived like that. You know he enjoyed…"

"Attention," Andrei said.

"If you wish to call it that." Rebecca's focus turned to Emerald. "And who is the lady?"

"Princess Emerald. Of Basilia. She is pregnant with my child."

Rebecca did not evince a very big reaction to the news. "Babies are good luck," she said.

Emerald wanted to tell her that it very much depended on the circumstances surrounding the pregnancy, but she didn't. She had a feeling that she did not want to be at odds with this woman.

The room they were standing in was a small, cozy kitchen, and the smells were enticing. This was the first time that Emerald had realized she was hungry. But it had now been several hours since her disastrous wedding, and she realized that she was still cold from being thrown into the sea, and now ravenous.

"Take the princess to your quarters. I will serve you both dinner soon."

She had never seen Andrei take orders outside a security capacity with quite such acquiescence.

"Who is she?" Emerald asked when they were out of earshot.

"She was… Our cook. A nanny of sorts. Like a grandmother. Who worked for us."

"You love her," Emerald said.

It came out more of an accusation than she had intended it to be.

"I'm not entirely sure what love is."

His words were a dagger straight to her heart. Andrei should know what love was. Because she'd loved him all this time.

Except you didn't show it to him, because you couldn't. So now it's all broken.

The house was like something out of a storybook. The walls were gilded, with ornate wallpaper. The stairs had luxe, patterned carpet. There were gold details everywhere, not like the palace in Alabria. It was more quaint. But in an opulent way. He pushed open the door and revealed a bedroom that was fitting for a fantasy princess, rather than for her.

Her own room at the palace in Basilia was quite modern. The one in Alabria had felt like a relic, but this was something else besides.

In the room was an ornately carved fourposter bed, with flowing swathes of fabric cascading down each post. An elegant canopy stretched over the top.

"This is lovely."

"I'm glad they fixed it to my specifications." His dark gaze flickered toward the back. "You will find that you have clothing there. If you wish to dress for dinner."

"Are you going to?"

"It is my first night as master in this home. Yes. I will dress for dinner. And I will see you there."

And with that, he walked away and left her, in this bedroom, in an unfamiliar home, in an unfamiliar country.

For the first time in her entire life, Princess Emerald felt stripped of everything. Her power, her status.

And perhaps worst of all, of any certainty in her relationship with the man that she had known for most of her life. The man she had always depended on. Trusted.

She was pregnant with his baby, and right now she had no idea what they were.

Or what would become of them.

Andrei knew he couldn't avoid the phone call when it came through.

He wasn't a coward. And when it came to this, he would face up to what he had done, even though it was going to destroy everything. He had known that it would. From the moment he had taken hold of her and carried her away, he had known it would. Hell, he had made that calculation when he had decided that taking her was the only thing that could be done. After he'd had her in front of the vanity, a punishment for them both, he had decided that they would both end themselves over this.

But that was before.

And now, there was this conversation.

He answered the phone. "Hello?"

"That's what you have to say to me? *Hello*. As if this is a call to discuss the weather, and not you taking my sister at the altar and causing an international incident."

"Is it an incident? We are blessedly free from the news."

"How nice for you. I am slowly boiling to death in the consequences. Lucian wants a war."

"There is nothing I can do," he said, realizing what he was saying. He did not think that Lucian would actually start a war over this. Perhaps a trade war. And he understood that there would be long-term consequences to that, but he had given up on the greater good.

There was only Emerald. Though his heart felt dark and scarred where she was concerned. Perhaps it had always been that way.

"Why did you do that?"

"I had to."

"Andrei, you have never done anything that would put our country at risk. You've never done anything that would put Emerald at risk. And so I am asking you, what insanity overtook you that you would steal her from the altar? Was Lucian a threat to her? Because I can accept that. If Lucian had put her in danger, then you did what you had to do. But there is nothing else short of that which justifies your actions."

"He was not a threat to her," Andrei said. "But she's mine."

"This is what I feared. Are you telling me that you… Did you lay a hand on my sister?"

"I laid more on her than a hand, Onyx, and I will admit that before a firing squad if it comes down to it."

"I trusted you."

"And I was trustworthy. Until I was not."

"This doesn't explain anything to me."

"I can't explain it to you. What happened on the yacht is between Emerald and me. The decisions that were made… You are a good friend, and a good king, Onyx, but you don't know everything. Not about your sister, and not about me. We have our own relationship, and have all these years." It felt disingenuous for him to say that now with all of the acrimony swirling inside him where she was concerned. But that was his business too.

"Are you going to marry her?"

"I haven't decided. There is the complicating factor of her pregnancy."

"What?"

"She's pregnant. The baby is mine. She was going to marry him and keep the child from me. I think you can see where that has put Emerald and me in a difficult position personally."

"If you harm one hair on my sister's head—"

"I won't harm her. But whether or not I marry her remains to be seen. But I will have my child, Onyx, and I will not let anyone or anything interfere with it. Until the child is born, Emerald stays with me. I will not have another man claim my son or daughter. Do you understand me?"

There was silence on the other end of the phone. "If you were here, I would cut off the offending member myself. I hope that I've made myself clear."

"You have. And I wouldn't blame you for it. In your position I would do the same. At least, I would if I had family. I don't. This child is the only family that I have. The only one I will ever have. She tried to take that from me. She knew that she was pregnant. She was going to allow Lucian to claim my child as his heir."

He knew Onyx enough to know that he was struggling with that. To know that he would find that as much of an affront as Andrei did. To know that he would not let that stand.

Whatever he said.

"You would claim your heir. Whatever the cost, you would claim your heir, and we both know that."

"You're a bastard who should never have gotten my sister pregnant in the first place."

"What happened between she and I is our business, but I will not allow you to labor under any sort of delusion that she was taken advantage of. I would never have touched her." That tasted like a lie. Because as they had gotten closer to Alabria, he had been tested to his breaking point. Emerald had pushed, and he had given in, but what would he have done if that hadn't happened? He couldn't say for sure, not now, not given what had happened in her room at the palace in Alabria, that he would've kept his hands to himself.

"I don't think that you would force yourself on her," Onyx said finally.

"Of course I wouldn't."

"Are you in love with her?"

"Whatever I felt for Emerald is clouded at the moment."

There was another long pause. "Where are you?"

"I cannot tell you that."

"For God's sake, Andrei, is there no trust between us?"

"No," Andrei said. "I can trust no one and nothing. Where we are is none of your concern."

He'd thought he could trust Emerald. He'd given her more of him than he had ever given to anyone. He'd sacrificed his honor at her altar to discover she'd betrayed him in a way he hadn't even fathomed.

"I can have your phone traced."

"You can't, actually, because it is blocked, because I am the head of your security, and not even you will be able to get the permissions to do that."

"Emerald is my world," Onyx said. "You would keep my sister from me, even now? She is pregnant with your baby and if she wants you, and doesn't want Lucian, then of course we can discuss this."

"I cannot. I won't."

"You are dead to me," Onyx said. "There is nothing complex about that."

"Then you can forget that either Emerald or I exist."

He hung the phone up and threw it down onto the floor, crushing it beneath the heel of his shoe. He did not think that Onyx would be able to track it. It was a completely blocked and protected phone. But if he was able to somehow break that, and find a location for it, Andrei wasn't going to assist him.

He buttoned up his black jacket and walked out of the bedroom, heading down to dinner.

His mood was black. And he almost felt sorry for Emerald that she had to deal with him. Except, she had created the situation.

He walked down the stairs, surprised at how much memory of this house was inside him. He hadn't realized. He didn't think about his home in Romania, at least he hadn't done so until he had needed it. Until he had needed to call upon the strength and ruthlessness of his father to save them both, and he'd thought that she would be happy.

He'd thought he would be, but the baby made it a betrayal in a way it hadn't been before.

And now… He knew it had been there all along. He had suppressed it, for honor. For the sake of duty. Because he felt that he owed Onyx fealty. Now? He would owe no one but himself. It was a devil's bargain, this. Embracing the poison of the Ardelean blood. Yes, it was a trap. And now that he had snared himself in it there was no going back. He had chosen this road. This path.

He walked into the dining room, and Emerald was already sitting there, dressed in green. He had specifically requested that they make as much of her clothing as possible green. He loved her and that color. At least he had. When he didn't look at her and see half enemy half lover.

"Your brother called," he said.

Her eyes went wide. "Is he…"

"Furious."

"I want to call him."

"Well, that will be difficult now, because I destroyed my phone. And so the two of us find ourselves here without a means of communication to the outside world."

"You're insane," she said. "I've known you for all these years, and you have never… You have never behaved this way."

"And *you* were going to pass my child off as belonging to another man. So, I suppose these are unprecedented times for us all."

"I didn't know what else to do," she said.

"And what you did was the wrong thing," he said.

"How nice of you to have such a clear view of it, as it affects you."

"And what other view should I have?"

"I asked him if he'd set me free. He said no. And as far as I knew you were gone, so what else was I supposed to do, Andrei? Free myself? Run past a gauntlet of guards?"

Her words affected him, and he didn't want them to. He wanted to stay in this space he'd gone to when he'd decided to capture her. This place that was filled with anger, justification for his actions. For his hurt.

"I've given up on duty. It's done. I burned it all to the ground. I made my choice. So you can sit there, in all your piety, and reflect on the good works that you would've done. And what good works they would have been. Pleasuring King Lucian, standing as his queen, bearing my child for him, and then more children for him besides. And did it make you feel good? Because you might think that you need a sense of satisfaction for your honor to get off, Emerald, but you and I know differently. You were well able to get off just with me. Knowing that it contributed to nothing, no good, greater or otherwise except the explosive desire between us."

"You are the *most difficult man*." Her face was red, her whole body rigid, vibrating with anger.

"And I can be more difficult, if it comes down to it. I would suggest that you don't try me."

"Do you think I'm going to make this easy for you? You don't get to take away my agency, my free will, my choices, and then have me simper at your feet. Is that what you think? That because of all this long-standing history between us I'll get on my knees and give you pleasure, thank you for rescuing me from my own choices?"

"You would, if you had any real idea of what I saved you from."

"Is that going to be what you use to make yourself feel better about all this? You're going to pretend that he's the monster everyone says he is."

"I don't care. He could be the best and kindest king in the history of the world—though we know he isn't—but you don't want him. I know what it's like to sleep with someone and to feel nothing but cold afterward. To feel further away from yourself, and who you are, and from any other person than you ever have. Because when you try to fill the deep, unending hole inside you that wears into you over time from unrequited need, all that you do is fill it with acidity and disappointment. Ask me how I know."

"So you claim you're saving me from a lifetime of bad sex?"

"You've only had good sex, Emerald. See, you don't actually know what a gift I've given you."

"Bastard."

"No. My parents were married when I was born. My mother was forced into it by my father. I won't force you into marriage. So our child very well could be a bastard. I would learn to keep my judgment to myself. Otherwise, look at what you're calling your own child."

"I don't know that I want to have dinner with you," she said, standing.

"Sit," he said. "This is not your brother's palace. It is mine."

She shocked him by obeying. He would've done nothing to her had she not. And she should well know that. But this was the trouble. She was compelled by him, even though she was furious at him. She wanted to be near him, even though she wanted to push him away. He knew that because it was how he felt. He wanted to spit all kinds of venom at her, and then he did want her to kneel before him. He wanted her with him, as much as he wanted to push her away. As much as he wanted her to feel a dagger in her chest, betrayal at his hand, as he had done with her. He wanted her near.

It frightened him how much that reminded him of his own parents. His mother had been forced into marriage. A trade between crime families, and she had loathed his father. But she had been helpless in the face of her desire for him. So much so that even he, as a child, had realized that. That there was a bond between his parents that neither of them seemed to truly want, but they couldn't escape either.

This house, this moment, this woman, reminded him of things best left in the past.

"And what is your plan?"

"To keep you with me until the child is born. Until

I can ensure that I have claimed the child, and no one else can."

"And then what do you do with me?"

"Again, that remains to be seen. Perhaps I will return you to your kingdom. And I will keep your child with me."

He was being a villain now, and he knew it. He didn't mean it, either. But he'd wanted to say it because it helped feed the dark, angry thing inside him.

Her face drained of color. "You can't do that. You can't take my baby."

"But you tried to take mine."

She looked down. "That was different. You wouldn't have known. You would never have known."

"And that makes it better?"

She shook her head. "No."

The doors to the dining room opened, and Rebecca came in, carrying a tray with a giant bowl on it, and two smaller bowls beside it, along with some rustic bread. This was not the kind of showy feast that was served in Basilia. But it reminded him very much of meals he'd had in the nursery. With the other children. Other crime lords' children. He wondered if any of them had survived to adulthood. If any of them had been able to decide their own fates. Or if, like his mother, all of the girls had been married off to dangerous, ruthless men. If, like him, the sons had been in danger of being collateral damage in a war, and if some of them had died before ever becoming men.

Likely.

They hadn't known it, not then. They'd had fun,

like other children did. Especially when they were able to be with each other. Rebecca set the terrine on the table and dished a helping of soup for him, and another for Emerald. “There is also bread and butter,” she said. Then she looked at Andrei for a very long time. “It is good to have you back. You are the image of your father.”

Andrei tried to smile. “Thank you.”

Then she turned and left them there. Emerald looked angry, but took a bite of soup, which turned into two, and then three, as she ravenously attacked it.

“Hungry?”

“Yes. I was stolen from my wedding and brutally dragged into the sea. It works up an appetite.”

“I would imagine.”

His own stomach growled, and he reached for the butter and the bread, lathering on a thick layer before dipping it in the soup.

The taste of home was undeniable. Strange. He wouldn’t have said that he missed this. That he missed Romania, or anything about the life he had before. But this reached down deep, into corners and memories that he hadn’t known existed still. This made him feel… Whatever the feeling was, he couldn’t say that he cared for it.

“You grew up here?”

“Partly,” he said. “My father had many residences. For many reasons. We would have people here to visit us, but they would have to switch modes of transportation to make it confusing. They would come blindfolded, guarded.”

"And they… Were okay with that?"

"I don't think you understand. What Boris Ardelean demanded, would be done. He was a dangerous man. And no one stood against him. Except for Luca Accardi. Leader of one of the largest crime families in Italy. He was the only one who dared go up against my father, and he had decided that it was his mission to kill him. And once he stood up against my father, so did many of the other families that we had called… Friends."

"Friends that were blindfolded."

"There is some honor among thieves, Emerald, but it is not a very nice honor."

"But you were only a boy. How were you aware of all of this?"

"It is part of being one of the children in these sorts of families. Particularly if you are the heir. We knew. We were hardened to the violence, to the danger from an early age. When your life is in danger from the moment you're born, and those around you make it clear, you become accustomed to it. Then, you have no fear. When you have no fear, you can be molded into the kind of man who can run that sort of empire."

"But your father was afraid. He ran."

"Yes, and only then did I realize my father might not be…immortal. But he knew, of course. If you are dead, you cannot continue to amass wealth." He was quiet for a moment, memories, feelings, impressions of a time long gone by filtering through his mind. "I do not think my father would have been proud of his death. I don't think he felt there was a risk in the crossing. Because he would've rather died in a hail of gunfire, that much I do know."

"Even as a twelve-year-old boy, that's your perspective?"

He nodded. "Yes. Even as a boy. Because he instilled a certain sort of bravery inside me. Because he taught me all that I needed to know. And he did that from the cradle."

"I don't want that for our child."

"Don't worry. I have no designs on picking up the reins of his criminal empire. I'm happy to let it die with him."

"Good."

"I do not have a need for power. But I will claim what's mine. That is a promise."

"I know that you… I know that you are angry with me but—"

"This is not a difference of opinion to be solved through a conversation, Emerald. You betrayed me. And I may not have designs on my father's criminal empire, but one thing I have in common with him is that I do not forgive easily. Or perhaps ever."

He was not capable of feeling guilt. He had thought that perhaps he was, but the way he felt in this moment proved to him that he was more like his father than he had previously realized.

A pity for them both. But a reality that he was beginning to embrace.

She finished the soup and pushed the bowl forward. "I find that I have spent as much time in your company as I can bear."

"Good night."

There was no reason for her to stay.

He might want to spend another hour or so in her presence, but why? It was only mutual torture.

The part of him feared that a lifetime filled with the mutual torture of wanting one another was going to be a hallmark of their relationship.

It had always been thus. And when they'd had each other, they'd shattered the world.

So back to this it was.

It was too late to change course now.

CHAPTER ELEVEN

She couldn't sleep. The bed was beautiful, and comfortable, and she was exhausted from everything that had happened in the last twelve hours, but she still couldn't sleep.

She was dressed in a soft gown that had been provided by Andrei, and part of her felt that she should perhaps resist his gifts. Resist wearing the clothing that he had provided for her, resist… The food, everything.

Except she couldn't. She was pregnant, and she needed to take care of herself. And also she just… The dichotomy of her feelings for him was overwhelming.

Because in many ways, he was still the man who she had loved for more than half of her life, and then suddenly he was a stranger.

The son of a crime lord. And he looked ruthless. Capable of doing everything his father had done and then some.

She lived in a world where blood was everything. Royal blood meant that you had a duty to the Crown, to the kingdom, to your people. She had long believed that her blood meant that she was destined to be like her mother. To do what she had done, did that mean that Andrei was always destined for this? For a sort of ruthlessness that defied morality?

And then, part of it… She had to take some responsibility for.

She padded out of the bedroom and walked silently down the halls, the carpet soft beneath her bare feet as she went back toward where they had eaten their dinner. Then she walked through that room and into the kitchen. She startled when she saw Rebecca, standing there in front of the oven.

"Oh. Hello," she said. "I'm just making raisin bread for tomorrow. It's about to come out of the oven. Would you like a slice?"

Emerald's stomach growled. "I—I would."

"Have a seat, dear."

Emerald did and watched as Rebecca moved efficiently around the kitchen. She took the loaf of bread out of the oven, and turned the loaf pan upside down. Then she busied herself grabbing some butter, putting the kettle on.

"Tea or hot chocolate?"

"I would… I'd like a hot chocolate," she whispered.

"Wonderful. That will be a nice late-night treat."

"Have you been working like this at the house even without Andrei here?"

"No. I received a message that the house was being opened up again, and I hoped it was for him. I came the week before to make sure everything was good for him. He was such a lovely boy."

She couldn't help herself. She laughed. "He is… A slightly different sort of man."

Rebecca made a regretful sound. "I was worried about that. I always hated that with the children who would visit. Eventually, they would become so hard. By the time they were fifteen almost all of them had killed someone on behalf of their family. An initiation into that life."

"Did you always work for families of organized crime?"

She shrugged. "It was often the most secure work here in this part of the world. I always served the Ardelean family. And so, the money that I have always gotten is blood money. Though, all of that changed when Andrei's father died. But he left us money. His staff was cared for in the end."

"That seems such a contradiction. That someone could be so ruthless, and yet remember the people who worked for him with so much loyalty."

"That is the attraction of it. You make for yourself your own kingdom, your own people, your own laws. And you offer fearsome loyalty in return."

"But it's all dangerous."

She shrugged again. "Life is dangerous. As I said, I think the most tragic part is watching the children lose their softness. Because the men in this world, they are so hard. The women too, some of them. Andrei's mother was a great beauty. He has the look of his father in his eyes, but, his mother's features. They fought bitterly, the two of them. And yet they loved fiercely. Or at least they were obsessed with one another."

Emerald's stomach turned. "That sounds like a terribly brutal way to love."

"I suppose it is," Rebecca said. "But then, I think none of them knew another way to be. I think none of them knew another sort of life. Except this painful, life-and-death allegiance." She set the cup of hot chocolate in front of Emerald, and then, slipped the loaf from the pan without using an oven mitt, her hands obviously toughened from years of cooking.

"Do you have a family?"

She shook her head. "No. I was devoted to the children who came here. When they left, I lost everything. I helped raise Andrei's father too. Andrei was different. He was kinder from the beginning. When I heard that he had escaped, when I heard the news of him being in your country, I rejoiced. I had hoped that it might make him less feral."

"I thought you said he was lovely?"

"He was. Lovely, and feral."

"Well, some of this is my fault."

"I find with passion it is often just messy." She slid a slice of bread in front of Emerald, who buttered it generously, the butter melting, pooling on the sweet bread, and she picked it up and ate it fiercely.

"Well. It's complicated."

"I'm certain. Something is making you sleepless."

"It could just be the events of the day."

"There is a library, just to the left of the dining room. You might find something to help you while away your sleepless hours."

"Oh. That sounds lovely."

"It is," Rebecca said cheerfully. What life must it have been, to serve generations of mafiosi, to constantly be around the fringes of so much violence, but to be the one providing softness, food for the children.

It was such a strange thing. Emerald hadn't had a life free of struggles. She had lost her parents, and it had affected her deeply. But her life was quite limited in its scope.

There were things she never had to consider, like how she would make money and survive without the aid of the Crown.

It made her wonder about the lives of the people who worked in the palace and Basilia. The people who worked in Alabria. She took a sharp breath, and thanked Rebecca for the sustenance before taking herself out of the room and determining that she would explore the library.

She still wasn't tired. No. In contrast, she was invigorated, her thoughts churning.

She wandered down the hall, past some rooms that were dimly lit, empty. It was interesting how many spaces were in this house that didn't look like they had ever been used. Or perhaps that was simply the result of the cleaning. And certain spaces hadn't found their use yet.

Would she give birth to their child here?

Just thinking about spending nearly nine more months cooped up here, with a man who despised her as much as he had ever wanted her, filled her with the improbable twins of dread and hope. Because on the one hand it was difficult to stand being in the same room as him at the moment. But on the other hand, for many long years he had been the person she cared for most, next to her brother.

It wasn't like it had vanished just because things were difficult between them now.

She was surprised to see light flooding out of the library into the hall, and she paused before entering. Then her heart froze.

Andrei was in there, sitting by the fire in a large armchair, holding a book in one hand.

It was as if he sensed her presence. He looked up, his eyes finding hers unerringly.

Like they always did.

"Sorry. I didn't mean to interrupt."

"You've interrupted nothing," he said, intangible emotion burning in his gaze. She could see it even from across the room. But he was, of course, never going to talk about it. Not going to admit it.

"I couldn't sleep."

"What a strange phenomenon."

"It must be strange," she said. "Being here." She was going to try to be nonconfrontational. She hadn't expected to see him again tonight, but she had. So it seemed like it would be best if she didn't start a row when the two of them were already exhausted.

The simple truth was, putting aside the events of the past few weeks, she had known this man since childhood. She cared for him. And—again forgetting that he was the architect of the current moment—he was back in his childhood home for the first time since before his parents had died. Confronting so many things that he'd never had to before.

She could perhaps find it in herself to simply connect with him. To do for him what she would've done had they not slept together. Had he not kidnapped her. Had they not eroded the foundation of all the care they had for one another in a single night.

"No stranger than anything else," he said. "I have been a man outside myself ever since that ship went down. Basilia was not my home either."

"It was," she said. "My parents cared for you very much. They chose to bring you in and make you part of the family. If they were still alive…"

"What?"

Longing expanded inside her chest. If they were still alive, things would be so different. If they were still alive she would never have sought the marriage with King Lucian. She wouldn't have had to. There would've been other treaties. Other ways that her father handled things.

Why do you think that? Do you really believe that Onyx isn't the king that your father was?

No. She did. But Onyx was young. Not even thirty yet, and he didn't have the time on the throne that her father had. If her father were a king now, fifty and with all that experience behind him, then things would be different.

They would all be different.

She wouldn't have felt so desperate and driven to do this ultimate thing to honor her mother. Everything would be different.

"But it was not my home," he said. "It was not my

destiny. This was, but I cannot even return here and find my destiny because it is gone."

"You said that you didn't want it."

"I don't. But it is not a real choice, is it? All of my father's legacies have been burned to the ground, Emerald. There is no less crime in the world. No less pain. Power vacuums are meant to be filled. And when one man falls, another rises. And so, many men have risen in the years since to take my father's place. And they have died and others have been reborn to replace them."

"It's exceedingly grim," Emerald said.

"Life is exceedingly grim. Or have you not come to understand that yet? Your parents were good people. They took in a half-drowned boy and it was not their responsibility to continue to care for me once I healed. But they did. And they are dead, just the same as my father, who never lifted a hand to save anyone or anything but himself."

"But my parents have a legacy," she said. "A legacy of kindness. Of care. Of sacrificing for their people."

He said nothing, but he looked around the room, and then at her. "And what is gained by that? So they can be written about in the history books, but where does that leave you?"

"I will go back and serve my country."

"Do you believe that your parents loved each other?"

She blinked. "Yes. I do."

"So was your mother's act one of self-sacrifice?"

"Yes. She couldn't have known what was waiting for her in the palace."

"It wasn't the Dark Ages. She had seen pictures of

your father. Certainly she knew that there was an attraction there."

"Well, I saw pictures of Lucian. And I went anyway."

"You have so romanticized martyrdom. It would do you well to romanticize the martyrdom that you will find here. Martyring yourself for your child."

She gritted her teeth. "You're blaming me for this," she said. "And I don't deserve it. You think that if you hadn't found out I was pregnant, you would've taken me here, and we would've what? Married, been blissfully honeymooning by now? Tangled around one another, saying sweet words to one another? No. Because the only thing that you are equipped to do, Andrei, is *long*. Pining is what you're most comfortable doing. For the things that you can't have. Now that you have me, you don't actually want me. Because there's something… Broken in you," she said, completely losing track of the rule that she had made not to fight with him.

She continued on at him. "You know how to want. Not how to have. You do not know how to experience happiness, joy. Nothing. And it suited you, to make me the object of your desire and have me ever out of your reach. I just tested the limits of your self-control, and I think that's what you're really angry about. Your lack of self-control put you in this situation. Because you would have let me go. If you weren't so jealous, because you had touched me, because you knew you had taken my virginity, then you never would've taken me from that altar. You would have enjoyed your life fantasizing that you love me better than he ever could. Better than he ever did, without ever actually having to do any of the loving. Because now that you have me, you despise me. That isn't just about what I did. That's about your own inability to feel."

She began to turn to walk out of the room, but he was lightning fast, out of his chair, grabbing hold of her arm before she could do so. "You do not speak of me that way."

"What? Don't speak the truth to you?"

"I don't love you," he said. "You are right about that. But I wanted you. I wanted you with such a ferocity that it made my bones ache, and the reason that I didn't take you was that I knew nothing could ever come of it. You speak as though I am afraid, I am not afraid. I did you a favor. I could never have offered you marriage. I could never have offered you what you wanted, not and continue to let you live the life that you had before. Princess Emerald of Basilia could not marry the son of a crime lord. There is no noble blood in my veins, there is only selfishness. But it didn't change because I have you. Lust is not love."

He had succeeded in hurting her, and she despised him for that. It shouldn't hurt. Not when he was lying. "You said that I meant the world to you."

"You have to understand what that means coming from a man like me. My own father never loved anyone or anything more than himself. That is the life I know. I know how to swear allegiance and loyalty to a cause. I am very good at that. You were my cause for so many years. And so, there was no more glorious torture than desiring you. Than desiring to break that vow that I made to protect you. To keep you safe above all else. Yes, that's who I am. A man who only enjoys the sacred because they are forbidden. And perhaps you are right about one thing. I was ill-equipped to *have* the forbidden. And now I do. But don't turn it into something more beautiful than that. Do not adorn it with the flowers of love, when it is only base, common lust."

She slapped him. She didn't even think. Her hand was flying through the air, connecting with his face. She had never committed an act of violence in her life. But she had loved this man. With all of herself. And he was doing his level best to dismantle it. To dismantle everything. Because not only had he taken away her legacy, he had taken away her ability to do the one thing that she had needed to do in order to sit secure in her place in her family tree as one who had done well, but he had taken away the strength of what had happened between them. He was destroying it. Undermining it. Making it into something that she knew full well it was not.

He held the side of his face, glared at her, his dark eyes filled with rage. But he did not make a move toward hurting her.

"What would your father have done?"

"He would've given you as good as you gave," he said. "But I have no appetite for hitting women. Even if they are spoiled brats."

"Yes, because the act of a spoiled brat is to sacrifice herself for the greater good of the country."

"You keep telling yourself that. But you stand there,

and you accuse me of not being able to have emotions. Are you any different? You have no idea what it means to be alive. No idea what it means to be human, apart from your sense of honor. And so what do you do now, Princess Emerald, if you have no one to live for but yourself."

"I have my child," she said. "I will live for them."

"So comfortable with a cause. You are but a vessel. For justice for your kingdom, for our child. What else are you?"

"Whatever I am, at least I'm not a monster."

Then she did turn, and he didn't stop her. She put her hand to her chest and tried to still her throbbing heart.

How dare he?

How dare he ask those questions and lead her down roads that she didn't want to go down. Because they were…

Because they were right. Because he was right.

He was her weakness.

She knew it.

He was her weakness, and he was the thing that had caused her to stumble.

And now… She had no honor left. She had been exposed to the entire world by now, she was certain. Because Lucian knew the truth, so undoubtedly he had announced it.

And where did that leave her? Here in this house, with this man, with… Nothing.

No greater good. No cause, no… Nothing.

All she knew how to do was to be of service.

He was right. She was a vessel for the legacy of another person. If she were very, very honest. She was living for the memory of her mother so that she could feel closer to her.

She was living for the memory of her mother so that she wouldn't fade from memory altogether.

And she had no idea what living for herself looked like.

Well, she did. Because she had done it once. That night on the yacht, when she had let Andrei have her. When she had given herself to him. To him and nothing else. He had become her mission for that night.

She laughed, wiping tears away as she went up the stairs to her room.

Look what he had done to her. What he had done to them both.

But there was a point where she had to take responsibility for this. And actually look at herself. At what she wanted. It was a terrifying question.

Andrei had been safe for her too. In much the way that he had been for her.

He had been a man that she could long for, desire, and never reach out and touch. The country was her one true love, and everything else was simply a game.

Except he wasn't.

She lay down on the bed, feeling dizzy with tiredness, and despair.

She was so… So terribly frustrated with herself.

She wished that she could escape her own body, fly about the trees. She wanted Andrei to be her friend again.

Except, he had never been her friend. He had always been a man who felt like he owed the Crown.

Just as she was a woman who had always felt the same.

They were both set pieces, being moved around by the whims of politics and the needs of a kingdom.

And now they found themselves alone, with only their humanity, and they were doing a very bad job of wielding it.

They were lashing out at each other. Hurting each other. Her hand still stung from where she had slapped him.

Why had she done that?

She didn't like this version of herself. This version of herself that felt so out of control. This version of herself that was being driven by emotion, rather than duty.

And yet, with all of that stripped away, with the Crown gone, this was what was left. She couldn't escape it. She had to contend with it.

Nothing had ever been more terrifying.

CHAPTER TWELVE

ANDREI WOKE UP sitting by the fire. The sun was filtering through the sky, and his face was sore from where Emerald had slapped him. Deservedly. He had slept in the library all night, though he hadn't meant to.

Was this to be their life? Their marriage?

He owed her better than that. He was angry, still, but… To what end?

And what was he angry at?

It wasn't her. Not truly. If they were going to raise a child together, then they could not live like this.

He had lost his grip on himself. He might've embraced aspects of his father's ways, but one thing he would not do was raise a child the way he had been raised. He would not raise his daughter to be a pawn. He wouldn't raise his son to be detached and deadly.

Emerald's family was royal, she had treated herself in much the way the mafiosi's daughters did. That grim determination to use what she had available to her to make things better for the family.

In her case, the country. And yet the end result was the same.

He got up and walked into the dining room. There

she was, seated already. Drinking a cup of warm liquid, and eating a pile of toast. "Good morning," she said.

She looked up at him, almost shyly. There was none of the antagonisms from the night before. "I'm very sorry that I hit you."

"It is nothing," he said.

"It wasn't nothing. It was a total failure of maturity on my part."

"I antagonized you."

"Yes. You did. But that doesn't mean that I get to behave that badly."

"Sleep seems to have restored some of your civility."

She nodded. "We've known each other too long to fall apart."

He made a short noise in the back of his throat. "I suppose so."

"I realized something. I don't know how to live when it isn't for the greater good. You are right about that. I am ill-equipped to handle my emotions because I have never allowed them to take center stage. That is… It's very difficult. And I don't know how to do this. So, I'm going to make mistakes. And occasionally be deeply unpleasant."

"I am always deeply unpleasant."

"You didn't used to be."

"I was doing my job."

"Yes. And part of your job was suppressing yourself, as a man."

He nodded. "I have long thought that it kept the world safe for me. Because if I carry elements of my father with me—and these last days have proven I do—

it is best to keep it under wraps. But I will not be like my father with our child. And to that end, we must find a different way of being, you and I."

She put her elbows on the table, put her head in her hands. "This is so complicated. Because even if we make peace with each other, we might have plunged my country into war."

"Trust Onyx. He'll figure out a way out of this. You and I must focus on each other. On our child."

"You very casually put all this on my brother."

"Only because I devoted so much of my life to him. Asking him to devote a small portion of his to me, to you, is not entirely unreasonable."

She looked like she was considering that.

"All right. So what are we… What are we to do then? We are just in hiding?"

"We have all of these grounds. We can do anything you like."

"I just need to rest right now."

"Fair enough."

He sat down at the table. "Have you experienced symptoms of pregnancy?" The question felt stilted and stiff, but that was fair enough, because so did he.

"Not really. Though, I might be having a little bit of nausea, extra tiredness. But it's very hard to say. You know, given everything else."

"Yes. I suppose so."

"I don't know what to do," she said.

"What do you mean?"

"Even when I went to university, I got a degree that was about making me the best leader that I could be for the country. It was never about what I wanted. Because there has only ever been one real thing that I thought I could do. I was destined to be a political leader."

"And is that what you want?"

"Well, I think I would enjoy being a diplomat more than a queen."

"I'm going to say this to you gently. You have done a terrible job with diplomacy between the two of us."

She laughed. The humor in the moment deeply unexpected.

"Well. Yes. I suppose I have."

"But that is what you would prefer to do."

"Yes. I got such a thrill organizing the marriage deal. And if it had just been a trade deal, I think it would've been such a triumph. I probably could have enjoyed playing games on Wall Street. Rogue trading deals and that sort of thing. I love it. The strategy. But, what I've loved always had to be within the confines of where I was headed."

He nodded. "Yes. Well. Becoming someone who guarded others was a stark contrast to what my destiny would've been had I simply stayed at my father's house."

"You would've taken over the crime empire."

He nodded. "A certain amount of brute strength, hypervigilance, all of that, was required. I suppose I've always used elements of that with security detail. But there has never been a thought given to what I wanted. It has always been about what is right."

"I feel the same. Neither of us knows how to be people, you know. We are just symbols." Symbols that had finally reached their breaking point, given in to their desire for each other, even though it had been a very bad idea. Imperfect, broken symbols, who now found themselves without a mission.

"I couldn't deviate from the mission," she whispered. "Don't you understand? I was so terrified in that moment, and so sad, and I just couldn't make a different choice. I could only do what I knew to do. Part of me felt like you would understand." Her throat went tight. "Because what am I doing anything for if I'm not doing it for Basilia?"

"I know that," he said, the admission heavy because he had been clinging so desperately to his anger and now he knew he needed to let it go. To listen to her. "I know you did not act with maliciousness. I know you didn't intend to hurt me."

"But I did. I hurt you. I'm very sorry. I didn't intend to. I didn't mean… It doesn't matter. I was thinking of everything in terms of the cause. Not the personal. And now that I've pulled away from it all, I can see that what I was doing was shortsighted. I would've left him."

"But not until he had you."

She nodded slowly. "I would've tried. But I know that I would've regretted it. I know that I would've called for you. Because you are right. I have idealized this. This idea of living for duty and honor. But I don't know how to live."

"These things that you love about your mother. You love them in hindsight. What did you love about her as a child? Surely it wasn't the things that she did for duty and honor."

"No," she said. "I loved her softness. Her laughter. I loved it when she read me bedtime stories."

"Your mother is not only a symbol."

"I know." Her eyes filled with tears. "But it's so hard to… You might remember her even better than I do."

"It is possible. My memory of her is that she was extremely kind. Extremely soft. If I'm honest, Emerald, you remind me more of your father. He was very determined. Always excited about another plan, a diplomatic gain. He enjoyed the game of it, but in a way that was always generous, and considerate of others. He was a very good man."

"Yes," she whispered. "He was."

"But they did live. They did have lives that weren't simply symbolism."

She nodded. "I do know that."

"Why don't you rest?"

The idea of rest was foreign to her. She was always doing things. Always spearheading a committee, starting another project.

"It feels… It feels wrong."

"It is not," he said. "You are having my baby, and I have thoroughly antagonized you. I would prefer that you took your rest."

It was his form of an apology. He had never truly had to admit that he was wrong before. And with her, he knew he had been. His treatment of her had been unfair. And had been about his own feelings. Not about her.

"Rest," he insisted. "And maybe, for the first time, try and figure out what it is you want."

* * *

She was beginning to feel lazy.

She had spent days lying in bed since that strange, conversation she had with Andrei. She felt tender, thinking about her mom as a human. As her mother. Especially thinking about becoming a mother herself. It made her think about legacy in a very different way. She'd made it less of a personal thing because really remembering her mother hurt.

Andrei had offered her so much insight into her parents, and he had been so kind and… She didn't know where it had come from.

She also didn't really know how to get deeper than that.

He was such a strange brick wall.

There was an inherent goodness to him, she was sure of that. But there was also difficulty.

The man was difficult.

Her feelings for him were no less difficult. The trouble was lying around like this, with no royal duties, with nothing, was that she had the opportunity to examine images of different kinds of futures. And there was one that she had never let herself hope for. Not really. One where she married Andrei. Where she had love. And maybe she wouldn't be written about. A princess who married her bodyguard. Maybe it was no kind of legacy. Maybe it would make headlines, but nothing deeper than that.

She had lived her entire life for what would happen after she died.

She had no idea how to live.

It was that thought that finally got her out of bed on a supremely sunny day, and outside. Rebecca told her that there were berries along the trail, and if she wanted a cake, she could go and pick some. So, she found herself out on a sun-drenched trail that wound through a field, picking fat, red berries and putting them in a basket.

It was a delightfully slow, rustic thing to do, and she had never lived a slow or rustic life.

It was strange to think that only a month and a half ago she had been boarding a beautiful yacht with every amenity she could want, and now she was in a crumbling manor without access to the internet.

Picking berries.

But without the input from the rest of the world, it was like she could finally hear herself.

"What are you doing out here?"

She turned sharply, startling for a moment, because that there would be anyone out here was a shock, and her first thought was that Onyx or Lucian had found her. But it was Andrei. Thank God.

"You scared me," she said.

"Sorry. I didn't expect to see you out and about."

"I'm tired of myself," she said.

He laughed. "It's a common malady these days, I fear."

"Are you tired of yourself, Andrei?"

"Yes. One thing that living for a cause gives you is the relief of the weight of your own humanity."

She had to laugh about that, because it was true.

All she was left with now were her own petty fears

and discomforts. Her desires, the things that she wanted, even if she shouldn't or couldn't.

It was exhausting. It was better, actually, to worry about things on a global scale, because her personal economy was far more troubling, and also, it felt even more out of her control.

"I'm picking berries for a cake, because that at least feels like something."

"Can I join you?"

"I would like that."

"We used to come out here all the time when I was a child. Pick berries."

"You and who else?"

"There were often children. Of associates of my father. It was such a strange childhood. There were times when we were left to our own devices, left to run wild. And other times…"

She looked at him. "What?"

"I don't want to spoil a beautiful day with things about my childhood."

"Tell me."

"My father saw it as his duty to prepare me to take over the family business. That meant that when there were people who needed to be… When violence had to be dealt out, he would ask that I watch. You get used to it. You learn to stop thinking about how much it must hurt the other person. Slowly, over time, it begins to kill your empathy. That's the idea behind it. He didn't want me to have empathy. He didn't want me to care what happened to other people. He wanted me to care only about the mission. And so I am very good at that."

It was such a strange thing to realize, that he had been shaped by something so dark and sinister, and yet it had turned him into a very similar person to her.

Her own parents had been sweet, lovely. Well-intentioned.

She wanted to honor them, and that was where all of her feelings came from.

His father had simply bent and twisted him into a vessel. One that could contain all the violence his family required.

And then he had transferred that, that loyalty, to her and Onyx.

"It must be really hard to be back here, actually."

He shook his head. "I have some of the nicest times of my life here. I cared very much about all of my friends. I think that is actually the difficult part. It was not a miserable childhood entirely. I suppose children are resilient and they are determined to create fun no matter what. But there were things that… There were things that were quite miserable."

"I wish I had known this about you."

"Why? It wouldn't have changed anything. You and I were always going to be bound by the rules we made for ourselves."

He was right. Only in childhood had there ever been any lightness for either of them. When she was a little girl, she hadn't thought about her legacy. It was only after her mother had died. Before that, she'd known what fun was. What dreams were. She had imagined a family like her own.

"If I'm honest," she said, "I suppose I probably did

romanticize the idea of marrying a stranger. Especially as I got older, because I did know that I would probably have to do a diplomatic union. Knowing that my parents had done it, it just made it seem like there was the possibility for it to be wonderful. Like there was the possibility for it to work out."

His eyes burned into her. "And your feelings for me?"

She took a breath, looked away, tried to ignore the soreness in her chest. "I learned to ignore them. Sort of. It was a separate thing. I wanted you, but I knew that I could never have you, so it was sort of… Its own kind of beautiful tragedy, I guess. But please don't call it lust. It isn't. It isn't just lust."

He nodded slowly. "I won't."

"Good."

They finished picking berries in silence, and then she was surprised when it turned out that the offer from Rebecca for cake meant that she had to bake it. She had never baked a cake in her life. "She tricked you," Andrei said. "She's done the same for me."

"You will help her," Rebecca said, which was how she found herself in the kitchen with Andrei, baking a berry cake, which was far less disastrous than it might've been, but perhaps a little more disastrous than it should have been. Especially given that they were two adults with decent educations and a fair amount of competency between them in other areas.

But the cake turned out lovely, and the lemon drizzle on top only made it that much better.

They had that instead of a proper dinner, and afterward, he asked if she wanted to go for a walk in the moonlight.

Was this what being a person was? Eating and baking and laughing. Going for walks because you could.

Not sitting at a table for ages, doing multiple courses, and observing formalities. Working on royal administration at all hours of the day. Not that there was anything wrong with that. With being busy.

But this, this slow slide into humanity was lovely.

The moon was full, and cast a glow on the overgrown garden, and she followed Andrei through the maze of paths.

"I bet you had a lot of fun in here when you were a child."

"Yes," he said.

He didn't elaborate. It seemed like the happy memories were almost as difficult for him as the painful ones. But then, she could understand how that was difficult. How it would pull you in multiple directions. Because it wasn't all bad. And it was so much easier when things could be absolute. So much easier when they could be clean. So bad that you wanted to wash your hands of them. So good that you wanted it to go on forever.

Maybe that was part of what she was looking for, living a life of duty and destiny. A cleaner, simpler life that didn't have all of this complexity. All of this potential for heartbreak.

And in a way, it kept her mother with her. But only as this simplified version of herself.

But it helped alleviate the grief that she felt over the

way she hadn't gotten to know her through the years. As an adult. As a woman.

Now she was going to be a mother herself.

She put her hand on her stomach. It still felt unbelievable.

She looked up at Andrei, the moon casting a glow on his features. Why was this so hard?

Why did neither of them know how to be together?

"This tree," he said, gesturing to it. "We used to climb up to the top, see how far we could see. Until my father put a stop to that. He thought it would help the other kids figure out the location of the house."

"You're kidding me."

He shook his head. "No. I'm not. He was an extremely paranoid man. As you must be when you sow the seeds of violence."

"You loved him, didn't you?"

"I…think so. Though I am not certain what love meant to me then, as I'm not certain what it means now, not inside me. I depended on them. I knew I was supposed to be like my father. I was in awe of him. My mother was beautiful, and volatile. I still carry grief for them, even though they were very flawed."

He reached up and grabbed the lowest branch on the tree. And then he hoisted himself upward.

"What are you doing?"

"Climbing. Because I can."

"I'm going after you," she said.

"No," he said. "You're pregnant."

"I'm pregnant," she muttered. "Not made of glass. I

don't intend to fall out of the tree. You know full well we climbed our fair share when we were kids too."

He kept on going, and she went after him. Until he stopped at a very wide branch that sloped out from the tree and neatly made a basket to sit in. She joined him there, their hips touching. It had been far too long since they had touched. Other than her slapping him, which really didn't count. And hadn't been good. What if they had met just like this?

Just as Andrei and Emerald. If he didn't have a crime empire in his lineage and loyalty to the throne, and she weren't a princess. It had never even occurred to her to imagine a different life. Her life was exceedingly privileged, and she did her best to live it with the knowledge of that. With gratitude. But right now, she resented it. Because what would life have been like if she could just be her?

No other baggage, no other responsibilities.

She leaned in and kissed him on the cheek. He turned to her sharply, surprise on his handsome face.

"That was an apology for the slap," she said.

"You already apologized for that," he said.

"I know. But… It was more than that. I imagine being up here with you all those years ago. If we were just kids, and we met, and there was nothing else."

"But there is something else. So many other things, and that will always be true."

"I know, but I just…"

"I don't want to be my father," he said, his voice stern. "Being here, being in this house it is…haunted.

By memories that are both good and bad. I find myself burdened by them."

"Why?"

"Because I loved him. And loving him was toxic. I won't be that for my child. We can find a way to fix this. A way to serve the greater good. We are good at that, Emerald, aren't we?"

"You just accused me of having no idea who I am if I don't have a cause."

"Perhaps…perhaps that is a good thing." He turned away from her. "Emotion in all its many forms is messy. Love is a liar. But we could unite and make this better. We could…we can fix all this. For us. For our child."

"I agree," she said, moving away from him, just slightly.

She did agree. But it hurt her. She'd been so happy with him a moment ago. So carefree and now she felt like she was losing her grip on that happiness. This felt more normal. More what she was used to. This distance. This need for a wall between them.

But what he said was true.

"We have known each other all our lives, and yet we don't know each other. We need to disentangle the difficult feelings between us. My father and mother's version of marriage was toxic. Twisted up in their lust, in all the sharp feelings. When I took you as I did in Alabria…"

"I wanted you."

He let out a rough sigh. "That isn't better."

Maybe it wasn't. Maybe her desire was sick. Maybe it was as damaged as they were.

She wished she knew how her parents had come to love each other. What they'd shared. But she didn't know because she'd been so young when they died. She had no blueprint. She had nothing.

Nothing except this ache inside her that she wanted so badly to make smaller. This ache that only ever seemed manageable when she was doing something. When she felt like she was fixing something.

These past few days here in the estate had been lovely, but she couldn't live like this. She had to keep moving. They had to make a decision about their relationship, because they couldn't stay here forever.

It wasn't what she'd wanted him to say. But she'd… slapped him. It had been wrong of her. It had been because of the way things were between them—so disordered and filled with…

Emotion.

He was right. They had a common duty. One to their child. That had to be the mission.

"We must call a truce," he said. "We are not enemies. We are to be parents."

She nodded. "A family."

He nodded, uneasy. "A family to me is difficult."

"It doesn't have to be. A family can be like mine. It can be happy. It can be…" She thought of her mother and father, laughing, reading to her and Onyx, holding them. The pain and anguish it created inside her almost took her breath away.

It didn't have to hurt. She would learn from it. Let her change her. Let it make her a good mother. A good…

"Let's take this time," she said. "This time here, to decide what we want to do. Together. As parents. For our child."

Because their child should be able to run wild and climb trees, and pick berries. Because their child should live in a home with parents who loved them. Who didn't fight. A mother who didn't lose her temper and slap their father. A father who didn't look at their mother with so much heat and outrage that it felt like they'd burn the whole house down.

She and Andrei knew how to resist each other. They'd done it for years.

If they could do it for the sake of the throne, surely doing it for their own child would be no more difficult.

Surely.

CHAPTER THIRTEEN

THE LIBRARY BECAME their neutral ground. They spent much of the day separate from one another, and Andrei felt that it was a decent testament to how they would manage everything once the baby was born.

He could imagine, very comfortably, the two of them having a life here. They would be… Friends, he supposed. Something so much less toxic than his parents. Throwing dishes, shouting, disappearing to their room for hours.

His mother crying.

His father had been particularly good at twisting the knife in his mother's ribs when he wanted to get a reaction out of her.

And his own love—as he'd known then, as he knew it now—served as a reminder of how emotions could be twisted and manipulated. He'd been so young. A vine that had been easily twisted around a trellis, to grow around the wrong ideas, feelings and conclusions.

It was only the royal family that had allowed him to understand love, but even then, in himself, he could not trust it. For good reason.

This place was so… Haunted. It held so many memories. Good and bad, and often the good and bad twisted around each other. He didn't want his child to grow up that way.

And that made him feel all the more resolved in this.

They took meals together occasionally, but tonight Emerald was having dinner in her room. She was having bouts of sickness at all times of the day.

She insisted that it was normal, and all completely fine. She was on a diet of herbal tea and extremely pungent pickled cabbage that made his stomach curl, but that she seemed to enjoy.

Or rather, craved, which she had informed him was slightly different from enjoyment, and had more to do with necessity.

He had been an only child. He had never really been around pregnant women. It was an experience.

He heard her behind him, and he turned. She was wearing a nightgown, barefoot, her red hair swirling around her shoulders. There were circles under her eyes, and he wished he could go to her and wipe them away. But he didn't.

Because that would be to break this spell between them.

Everything was good right now, and he didn't want to break it.

"And how was your day?" she asked, floating into the room and moving to sit in his chair.

A little quirk of hers. Or, she was trying to be annoying. The thing that was really annoying about it was that he found it cute, and he supposed it was okay for him to find her cute. Maybe they would coparent. Maybe they wouldn't even be a couple.

The thought of that made him taste something metallic in the back of his mouth.

"Fine. I did some work."

"What work do you do exactly?"

"I have investments. Mainly in companies that make military grade weapons."

"That sounds…"

"Like the most legal way to be adjacent to the kind of work my father did? You would be correct. But I understand it."

"It wasn't a judgment. I help run a country. I understand how these things work. Or I guess, I did run a country. Who knows what will be there when we get back."

"Well, nothing catastrophic has happened so far. Though the headlines about this are hysterical."

She narrowed her gaze. "You have internet access and you've been keeping it from me."

"Not consciously. But, I did figure it might only upset you."

"That's not for you to decide," she said, sniffing.

"I would disagree, Emerald. As I have brought you here to protect you. In all the ways that I can."

"Yes. Well. I do feel quite wrapped in silk."

"Good. You should."

She wrinkled her nose. "It's a bit weird to have you be this nice to me."

"It's better than the alternative."

"I know. I am very sorry that I slapped you."

"You don't need to keep bringing that up."

"No, I just… You're right. Things don't have to be like that between us. And I understand."

"Your parents seemed to have such a nice marriage," he said.

"Yes. And they were strangers when they met. It's so funny, because I know that in the modern world that's a very strange experience. But in the grand context of history, it's not. It's the way things used to work. And they made a lot of happiness out of it."

"My parents didn't. Or rather they had… Excitement. I fear very much that my mother loved my father more than he loved her. But then, I'm not certain my father loved anything more than he loved himself. No, I know he didn't. Because in the end, he held on to his position in the crime family for far longer than he should have. He should have gotten out earlier. He should've done something to save my mother. To save himself. Something more than running as he did."

"It probably wouldn't have changed the outcome."

"Maybe he would've been able to get safer passage if he hadn't been taking the only vessel available."

"And maybe my parents could've taken a different route. Left five minutes later. Not gone out at all. We can't know these things. And the truth is, you probably don't even have a clear view of your parents' marriage. That is the terrible thing about being young when your parents die."

He laughed. "My parents were not the king and queen of a country. I guarantee you I have a distressingly clearer review of who they were than you do of your parents. Also remember how old I was when I realized what they did in their room with the door closed for so many hours. They would have meals delivered and not come out. Marathons. I mean, I knew, but I didn't fully understand."

"Goodness."

"And my father was not soft with her. Or kind. It was… barbs. Coldness. It was… Extremely painful to be around, even as a young child who didn't fully understand."

"I'm sorry."

"It was much like his relationship with me. We would go outside and play catch. He could be warm and fun. And then he would bring me into witness the beating of a man who owed them money. And would tell me that I needed to get used to it, because it was the reality of running a business."

"Oh… Andrei. That is terrible."

"It was my father. Darkness and light. Good and bad. And God help anyone who loved him. Honestly. I don't want to be like him. I told myself that I needed to be. To claim you. I… I cannot subject either of us to that. But most of all, I will not subject our child to that."

"You're not him."

"I can never trust that. What I know is that my feelings cannot be trusted, and cannot lead. I need to…"

He looked at her, his gaze locked firmly on hers. He wanted to stay here because he felt like he had all the power here. Because there was no king but him. He was God in these mountains, and he did not have to deal with Lucian or Onyx, or the responsibilities that Emerald had in her real life. But that wasn't realistic. And it wasn't the right path.

That was the sort of thing his father would do. Consolidate his power. Protect it above all else. Damn his wife, and damn his child.

Damn them all to the same level of hell that he was destined for.

He couldn't do that. He had made the decision to keep things… Platonic with Emerald.

To keep from descending into that madness that had captured both of his parents.

But now he had to answer that dark part of himself. The one that wanted to keep her here. Keep her away from everyone.

His child was royal, even if he was not. Emerald loved her country.

And there was more to life than this compound. That was the life the child of a crime lord had to lead. Locked away, with so many enemies beyond the walls that you were never truly safe. All because of your father's ego.

He was still acting from a place where his ego was making decisions.

Especially with Emerald, and his refusal to marry her.

"This cannot endure," he said.

Emerald looked at Andrei, certain she was misunderstanding him. "What can't?"

"We are in hiding here, and it is sadly far too much

like the last couple of years I spent with my parents. I will not do that to my son or daughter."

"What are you…what are you proposing?" she asked, the calm, tranquil feeling she'd had a moment ago turning into something cold, afraid.

"I think we need to go back. Face all of this. Face all of this mess."

"And what if Lucian orders your death?"

"Come now, Emerald. I would not be so easily defeated. I would not be defeated at all. Do you not know me?"

"I do. You're arrogant and difficult and… I don't want the father of my baby to die."

She didn't want him to die. She didn't want to say that. Not now while he was in this space of cold, remote detachment.

"We need to marry," he said.

"I thought you weren't…"

"I don't wish to force you. You will not be my mother. I will not be my father. But I think it is the only way forward."

So logical. And correct, if she was honest. But it hurt all the same.

"Are you proposing a marriage in name only or…"

"For now," he said, his tone rueful. "There is no way for us to manage all the things we must if we let ourselves get lost in lust. That is what harmed us in the first place."

He was taking a lovely moment and turning it into something so cold.

He was right, though.

She didn't know what to do with all the feelings inside her, so big and unwieldy. She didn't know how she was going to be a mother, a princess, a wife. And the idea that they had a problem to solve together—that felt manageable.

Sorting out the issues between them much less so.

"All right, Andrei," she said. "I will marry you."

It had nothing to do with love, passion or desire. Nothing to do with what they'd felt for each other before everything.

What a strange realization.

He'd cared about her more before they'd ever made love.

Now…

Now there seemed to be nothing there at all. He'd locked it down inside himself, closed it behind him.

Now when she looked at him, she could see nothing but duty and honor. She'd hurt him with hers. Now he was killing her with his own.

"Good. We will travel back to Basilia tomorrow. You will speak to your brother. Leave Lucian to me."

CHAPTER FOURTEEN

WITH EMERALD SAFELY deposited in Basilia, he decided to make the journey to Alabria. She was resistant to the idea, and she was angry. But she needed to deal with Onyx, and her position in the country in her own time. He would not allow her to face Lucian.

Ever.

If the man were any kind of threat to her, then Andrei would kill him with his bare hands. Given the situation they were already in, that was probably only going to make things worse.

And he had to fix this. For their future. For their child.

They had found a way to be together back in Romania. He could imagine long, happy days, and no, perhaps they couldn't have everything.

Because of who he was. Because of the blood that flowed through his veins. Because of the way he was shaped by the cloistered world his father had raised him in. But they could have this.

They could have a family.

A better version of it than he'd ever had.

He could make peace with Onyx. And he was determined to do so.

But everything had begun to unravel when they had introduced sex, their own desires, their messy feelings. And in the time since then, they had found something more.

Something deeper.

Something that existed beyond the pining and longing the two of them had managed to make their entire identity.

He'd suppressed his need for her for years, and though he'd let it out, allowed himself to get swept away by it for a time, he could suppress it again. It would be better if they could go back to that neater, simpler way of being.

He took a small, faster ship to Alabria, cutting the journey down to one day, and by the time he set foot on the island, he was prepared for whatever met him.

If he died, it would be in the interest of keeping Emerald safe. And she was ensconced with Onyx, so she would be protected.

He walked up to the front doors of the palace and was greeted by the guard.

"King Lucian is expecting you."

"As he should be. Is there an executioner with him as well?"

"He's interested in what you have to say. He thinks you're brave. And mad."

"Perhaps," he said.

He allowed himself to be escorted into the throne room. They searched him for weapons. He wasn't that foolish. If need be, he would fight for his life with his bare hands.

He himself was a weapon. He didn't need to carry one.

If they had known this, perhaps they would've bound his hands. But they did not.

The king was sitting on the throne much as he had been the first time Andrei had laid eyes on him. With the sort of lazy indolence that many would see as non-threatening. But he saw it for what it was.

Lucian himself was also deadly. And there was no disinterest in him whatsoever.

He was languid. Like a cat ready to strike.

"My bride thief. Here you are. I didn't expect for you to return to me of your own free will. Do you have my chosen queen with you?"

"No. That is what I have come to discuss with you. I intend to marry Princess Emerald."

"That is a problem for me. Given that I've planned an entire wedding for the two of us. Once you monogram things, they don't let you return them."

"I feel that with the treasury as great as yours, whatever is monogrammed on your linens is not truly your main concern."

"Perhaps not. But I don't like to lose."

"What I propose to you is not a losing proposition. We can make something work."

"So say you. But what if I do not like what you have to offer."

"Reject it. Cut off my head. Promise me, whatever you do, you will leave Emerald out of it."

"I can make you a promise, Andrei Ardelean. But there is no guarantee that I will keep it. I am not a man of my word, nor am I a man of honor. Though, neither are you. I have done an extensive amount of research into your background since you took my bride. You are the son of a criminal."

"That is like calling a battleship a rowboat. My father was *the* criminal."

"Yes. So I read." He leaned forward in his throne, suddenly keen. "It was brave of you to take her like you did. And the spectacle. I enjoy a spectacle. I do not like finding myself without a bride, though. And I was publicly humiliated."

Andrei lifted an eyebrow. "You did not think that you would be publicly humiliated if people found out that she was carrying another man's baby?"

"No one would've ever discovered that."

"Really?" He snorted. "Can you be that naive? I heard that you were a great terror. And yet, your perspective on this is giving… Babe in the woods. Do you not think there would be speculation? Do not think that somebody would try to sneak a DNA test? Anything to undermine you in your power?"

"Why would anyone do that?"

"You are hated. Reviled. You are also blond, and Emerald is extremely pale herself. The chances of the child coming out looking very much my coloring should be a concern for you."

"A good point."

"Besides, you strike me as a despoiler of virgins. And Emerald is not that."

"I do enjoy a good despoiling." He looked thoughtful. Andrei was mindful of the fact that he could not make any of this too much his idea. King Lucian was the sort of man who liked to believe that everything was his own decision. Andrei didn't have to know him to know that.

"Find yourself a new bride. Get her with your own child, avoid the incident."

"I do suppose this adds to my lore. I also like that. As much as I enjoy spectacle."

"Did you murder your wives?"

He smiled. Just slightly. "No."

"Why is it you allow the rumors to persist?"

"I told you. I like a spectacle. And I like for people to not know which direction I'm going to come from. It suits me. I don't give a shit about my reputation, honestly. But I do care about somebody making a threat to my throne. And its sovereignty. And you present a good point about the heir. What will you offer me in return? For you have cost me a lot of money and trouble."

"Military alliance. Trade alliance. Everything that Emerald promised you. In addition to that, one of the things that I do in my own time is invest in new military technologies. If you would like to have access to the newest and latest advancements… They can be yours. For significantly reduced rates."

"Free," he said.

"If it pleases the king."

"Very little pleases the king. I am bored. And one thing I will say about the most recent events, is that they were not boring. I have no taste for killing you,

Andrei Ardelean. You will make a good ally, and an even better enemy. So, I would prefer that you stay on this side of the ground."

"Don't expect an invitation to my wedding."

"I wouldn't go anyway. It would be a terrible black mark on my reputation if I were seen as being the bigger person. I'll send a gift."

It rather felt more like a threat than an offer, but then most things of King Lucian did.

"I'll look forward to receiving it."

He was done. And now, all that was left was to plan the wedding.

"I was worried about you."

Emerald was awash in anxiety waiting to hear what had happened with Lucian and Andrei. She was worried for his safety. She…

When she had arrived back at Basilia, Onyx had given her some reprieve. He hadn't demanded an explanation immediately, but today, all bets were off.

"I'm sorry," she said. "I wasn't the one who spirited me off to Romania with no means to contact you."

"What were you thinking? Why would you decide to marry Lucian when you wanted Andrei?"

"Because I had decided that I couldn't have him."

"Why?"

"He isn't royal."

"That is high level bullshit, Emerald. I certainly never told you that you had to marry a man with royal blood. I never even suggested it. Andrei is my best friend. He is the most trusted man—he was the most trusted man—in my employ. I would have given you to him happily."

This was what she had been afraid of. This conversation.

She realized that now, as her brother looked at her with confusion and ferocity in his eyes. He would have allowed them to be together. Of course he would have. He didn't demand that she make something more of herself. He wanted her to be happy.

She was the one who hadn't been able to accept it. She was the one who had been fleeing these feelings for Andrei, and now she was stuck in this great and terrible middle ground with him, where there was something of a truce, but no more passion.

It was her own fault. It was her own fault because…

She tried to take a breath.

"But I wanted something more. I wanted to make something out of myself. I wanted…" She closed her eyes. "It made me feel close to Mom. This idea that I was going to have a dynastic marriage. One that changed something. I just… I wanted to be like her. Because I can't know her. I can't be with her. And if I have to accept that, that I just have to accept the grief. It's just so horrible. It's endless. And I…"

"The past is undeniably tragic," Onyx said. "For all of us."

"Yes." She looked at her brother, who had a remote expression on his face. She knew he missed their parents. She knew he loved her. But he could be so detached sometimes, like it was what he had to do in order to be king.

But she wished sometimes it wasn't that way.

"I do not give this my blessing," Onyx said. "He kidnapped you. He forced you down the aisle. You are clearly in a state."

"I'm not asking for your blessing. I'm just asking you to… Be my brother. While I try to figure out the situation that I've gotten myself into."

"I am always your brother. You always have me."

"And Andrei?"

"He and I will take some time before we repair our relationship. He took you away from me. He put you in danger. He didn't tell me where you were. He didn't trust me. It will take time for me to get over that."

"And fair enough. But he is the father of my baby."

"And he is that simply through donation of genetic material. To be called a friend is something he will have to earn his way back to."

The doors to his study opened, and Andrei came in. She had to fight the joy in her chest, fight to keep from flying out of her chair and into his arms. That wasn't the relationship that they had. They decided. It was for the best.

"It is done. He has agreed not to pursue any type of retaliation. I've made military alliances with him in exchange. And offered him technology."

"You don't have the authority to make those deals," Onyx said.

Andrei looked at him, hard. "Would you like to make this more difficult than it needs to be?"

"You need to remember who you are," Onyx said.

"I know who I am," Andrei returned. "I know who I

am, and I have taken steps to ensure that I will behave with honor either way. I am going to marry your sister. Whether we receive your blessing or not."

"She and I just covered that. I do not extend my blessing, but I will not stop it from happening."

She hated this. The feeling of the rift between them. He was a mess, and she knew that, but she shared the blame. She'd been a coward when he'd needed her to be brave. She had been resisting her feelings for Andrei to protect herself.

And now… All this had happened. It was such a huge mess that needed cleaning up.

But at least they had started. As for the issues between the two of them? She didn't know that it would be so easy.

"How quickly do you suppose we can plan the wedding?"

"It should be easy enough," she said.

"With my money?" Onyx asked.

Andrei turned to him sharply. "I will pay. It does not have to be a royal wedding. We can have it anywhere."

"Don't be a fool. I will pay for it. She's my sister. It is a royal wedding. And it will be here. I may not be giving this union my blessing, but one thing I will not tolerate is you being an idiot."

Andrei almost laughed. "Then you see it done how you wish, Your Highness."

"I have moved your quarters," Onyx said. "You will be in the same wing of the palace as Emerald. A suite of rooms is my gift to you."

"We won't be living here full-time," Emerald said softly.

"Of course not," said Onyx. "But still, that is my wedding gift to you. Not that you'll be needing it."

It was Onyx who stormed out of his own office, leaving her there with Andrei.

The tension stretched between them, her desire to close the gap between them increasing. But she couldn't. She had made vows to him in Romania. About how this would be.

"I'm glad that you're all right."

"I'm quite relieved."

"Onyx is going to be a little bit more difficult."

"I'm not worried about him."

She was. She hated this. Hated the distance between them. Hated the distance between herself and her brother.

"I hope so."

"We have a mission, Emerald. And we are most of the way to completing it. Do not lose hope now."

She shook her head. "I won't."

"Good. This is why we will succeed."

"Of course. This is why we will succeed."

He nodded his head and left the study, and Emerald found herself sitting there by herself. The same room where she had first told her brother that she was going to marry Lucian. The same room where all of this had begun.

She did not feel determined at all right now. She felt defeated.

She had created this problem. Fixing it would be ugly, and Andrei wouldn't like it, That much she knew.

But one thing she also knew about herself was that she was strong enough to do it.

She had loved Andrei Ardelean for all these years. She wouldn't give up on them now.

CHAPTER FIFTEEN

THEY MANAGED TO mostly avoid each other in the lead-up to the wedding. It was for the best.

Andrei found that the ache he felt for Emerald never fully went away. He would learn to live with it. To make the pain part of breathing. The ache a part of himself.

They had made their decisions, and they were the right ones.

There was difficulty between himself and Onyx, and that was all the challenging emotion he could handle right now.

The truth was, he had to figure out how to be a father, when the one thing he knew was that he couldn't be his own. His own feelings for his father were so complicated, so tinged by trauma and loss, by who his father was, that it was difficult for him to figure out exactly what that meant.

If he hated his father it would be so much easier.

He was trying to find his way to that.

The door opened behind him, and he turned. Emerald was standing there, looking at him, her expression tentative. "Can I come in?"

"Of course. This is your room as much as it is mine."

Except they were like that. They didn't have that intimacy.

"It can't be like this for our entire marriage," she said.

"What exactly do you mean?"

"You know that it can't be. We aren't going to be able to resist each other. Not for the rest of our lives. It simply… It's going to end up making more problems than solutions. That's all."

"Emerald, this is dangerous." Everything in him was shouting to run away. After what had happened between them the last time they were together, the monster that had been awakened inside him…

"No," she said. "What's dangerous is us denying ourselves. Look where it got us. It almost started a war, and it certainly started one between the two of us. But we've…we've created a friendship since then. We need to trust ourselves."

Her hands were shaking, her eyes hopeful. If he denied her now, he would hurt her.

And the truth was, he didn't want to deny her.

He burned for her. His entire body shook with the need to touch her, hold her, take her, whenever she was near, and yet he knew he couldn't risk it.

This was a war he'd wage all his life, but the resistance of it would be the proof that he could be better.

Stronger.

"I can't see a future where neither of us ever wants a lover," she said.

Never.

There would never be anyone but her.

"And we may want more children," she said. "Besides, as unhealthy as your parents were, won't we be just as dysfunctional? Denying what we want and..."

His strength ran out. Was there another way? His mind and body were working as quickly as possible to try and make a new bargain. To try and find a new way to be.

A way that would allow something. Just a touch, perhaps. A taste.

He wouldn't lose himself.

He reached out, taking her chin between his thumb and forefinger, holding her steady as he leaned in to kiss her. Different than any other kiss they'd ever shared. It was slow. Methodical. There was no desperation. It wasn't like they were trying to outrun a clock. It wasn't because he was trying to punish her.

It was just a kiss. And there was something beautiful about that. It was a kiss, because they both wanted it. And who knew what it would mean later. It felt good now.

Emerald, and Andrei.

There was no Basilia. There was no Alabria. There was only this.

He picked her up and laid her down on the bed, glorying in the need that was building inside him.

This felt different from what had happened before.

Where the first time had been glorious and painful, aching because it was going to be all they had, and that night at the castle had been her punishment. This was an attempt to rebuild. Not tear down.

This was who they might have been if they'd been free from the beginning to choose who they wanted to be.

He kissed her. This wasn't hurried. It was a slow exploration. His lips over hers, his tongue thrusting deep, sliding against hers, a leisurely tasting.

His heart was beating fast, and he reached down between her legs and pushed his fingers beneath her underwear, feeling how slick she was between her thighs. Oh she wanted him.

He wanted her more than he could possibly say. More than sanity. More than keeping his word. He wanted to go faster, and he wanted to linger in this moment forever.

She pulled at his shirt, and he let her draw it up over his head. Then he reached around and unzipped her dress, tugging it down, exposing her body. She wasn't wearing a bra, only a pair of very brief underwear, and he dispensed of those two quickly.

Still, he just held his body against hers, kissing her. Indulging himself.

She moved her hands over his shoulders, his muscles, helped him take off his pants, everything else. She explored him, kissing her way over the acres of muscle, all of his skin.

And he returned the favor.

Committed the taste of her, the shape of her, to memory.

What if they could have this?

He was on fire with that realization that they could. They had already abandoned everything. They had already burned it all to the ground. They'd rebuilt into this, so why not have this? Why not have each other?

Why not try?

Maybe they didn't know how. But they could learn. They could learn, and then they could always, always have *this*.

She gasped as he kissed her neck, moved down to her breasts, down her stomach, between her thighs, where he feasted on her. She was the most glorious dessert he'd ever had. All slick and sweet like honey. He wanted to gorge himself on her forever.

He wrapped his arms around her, pulled her up into a sitting position, her knees on either side of him. She lowered herself down onto his stiff, aching staff, taking him in slowly, inch by excruciating inch. She gripped the back of the headboard, their eyes locked on one another's. As she rode them both toward oblivion.

She flexed her hips back and forth, then rose up slightly, the feel of her tight wet body around him almost sending him over the edge into oblivion.

She established a rhythm that carried them both over the edge, and when he tightened his hold on her hips, and thrust up inside her, shouting her name…

She was his.

His.

No. He couldn't throw himself into this. He couldn't lose himself.

He couldn't.

He wouldn't deny them this. Wouldn't deny their desire for one another, but it would never be more than that.

It was a good thing.

Because he would never be a father like his own. A father who chose to hurt his son in service to power. A father who would choose wealth above all else, including the safety of his family.

It could never only be the two of them. It would always be the weight of her crown—a weight she had chosen. And the weight of his past.

No amount of desire could overcome it.

He had surrendered to her here. Solidified his own weakness.

He pushed her away from him, his blood raging. "This cannot happen."

"Andrei…we can't…"

There was something wild inside him, a need to push her away he couldn't articulate or fully understand. He wanted her gone, away from him. He didn't want her testing him, he didn't want to face his own weakness.

His own vulnerability.

"This is nothing but part of a plan for you," he growled, the lie on his tongue tasting like acid. "Carefully plotted to make your legacy, your life, look better. Get out."

She stumbled off the bed, naked, beautiful.

Wounded.

She was the promise of something he wanted. Something he'd always desperately wanted.

But it would never be his.

"We will marry tomorrow," he said, his grip on his control slipping. "And we will kiss at the altar. But I will not touch you again."

CHAPTER SIXTEEN

HER BROTHER TOOK her arm just outside the church. It was an echo of her aborted wedding two months ago, and it was painful now to think of how different things might have been if…

And Andrei had the power to destroy her. He always had.

He had nearly done it last night. Her attempt at finding a way to make things easier. To make them better.

Because you still haven't told him the truth.

You haven't told yourself the truth.

What she felt for him was so big that it had always felt like the right thing to run away from it. It had always felt safer and better to turn toward duty, rather than surrendering to what she felt for him.

And now it was too late. Because the fire between them had turned into something uncontrollable, unbearable, kerosene on a little match when she had decided to marry Lucian after being with him.

He had sacrificed everything for her. To be with her. He had given up on his duty. He had embraced the thing inside himself that scared him the most, and she hadn't. She hadn't offered him anything.

She had chosen duty over the desire that existed between them, but not because it wasn't strong for her, but because she was afraid of it.

Scared enough that the idea of marrying a man she didn't love, a man who was potentially cruel, a man who was potentially a murderer, seemed less frightening than submitting herself to a future loving Andrei. Needing Andrei.

Because when you needed people, they died.

And all that was left was their memory.

All that you could cling to was… Grief.

Unless you could make it a mission. She was so good at making a mission.

And so bad at living. At feeling. At being a whole person.

"What is it?"

"It's too painful. I can't bear it, Onyx. I can't bear how much I love him. I haven't been able to bear it or stand it or admit it since I was fifteen. If I were to lose him, I would lose everything. Love is terrible. I pretty much went to the ends of the earth to outrun it, and it came after me."

"Then why do you look so sad? If the two of you love each other…"

"Because we don't. Because it… I love him. I do. But I don't know how to reach him. I don't even know how to reach myself. It sounds so stupid, but I only know how to be a princess. In Romania, it was different. I was… Angry, and sometimes unstable. I was his friend. Then we decided that we would do this, for the good of our child. We are better when we're on a mission, don't you get it?"

"I don't. I've never been in love."

It spoke volumes about his marriage. He wasn't even trying to hide it. She wondered how things had been in the months since she and Andrei had left. The answer was likely, not good. Not good at all.

"Well, it's terrible. I… I hurt him. I think he did love me. I don't think he ever will again. Our relationship is now in name only."

"That is the most foolish thing I've ever heard," Onyx said. "And guaranteed to end in destruction."

"It won't. We're both very good at this."

"Let's not discuss the severe implosion the two of you had right before your wedding."

"I'm sorry. That's really what I'm trying to say. I'm sorry. I am going to marry him. Our child will be legitimate." Since she was making demands now, she would go ahead and make more. She still wanted to do something of importance for her country, and she would. "And I would like a job in your cabinet. I would like to take on foreign affairs. I know that I can negotiate different trade deals, different alliances. I'm good at that."

"You are. You know you could've always had this, if only you would've asked."

"But I was being the architect of my own impossible love story," she said. "I couldn't ask you for this, I couldn't take it, because then… I wouldn't have any excuses, and how can I keep myself safe?"

"And how will you do it now, sister? How? Because you will have everything you want, and still deny yourself? You will have the man of your dreams, be married to him, have a child with him, and deny yourself everything?"

"I'll have him. With me. That's not denying myself everything. The worst thing is to miss somebody like you've lost a limb. At least to have him with me."

"Hear me when I tell you this. There are worse things than that. Having somebody with you and not being able to reach them, that is the loneliness that you are not prepared for."

It felt like such a deep, dark warning, and it left her feeling shaken.

"Well, it's something I'm going to have to get used to, I fear."

"You don't have to get used to it, Emerald. You can still turn back from this. I don't care if there are two thousand people out there and millions on a live stream. Nothing has ever mattered but your happiness."

It wasn't a shock to hear that from her brother. He had always behaved that way. It seemed like she was the only person who had a difficult time wanting to be happy. Because happiness on a grand scale felt so risky. It felt like something that could be taken away. Felt like something awful, painful and terrible.

"You can turn back."

She was in a terrible position now. Because the truth was, she could never fully be happy without Andrei. He was her person. In so many ways. But now that she was looking straight down the barrel of her own cowardice, she realized that there was one thing she hadn't offered him. Her heart.

She had offered her body, she had offered her hand in marriage, but she hadn't truly made herself vulnerable to him.

He had done it for her.

He had risked everything to take her from that wedding. He had shown his heart. Because he hadn't been claiming the baby. All of his anger and his rage after that had been because he had broken his own moral code, his own vows, for her.

Why would he say that he loved her after that?

He had been willing to break himself in half. And then, he hadn't been.

But if he understood that it came from a place of fear… Because her feelings were so strong, not because they weren't strong enough.

She gripped her bouquet of flowers tightly, and held on to her brother's arm.

"You love him."

"Yes."

"And you don't think he loves you."

"Not anymore. I feel like everything inside him retreated. And why wouldn't it? You don't know everything about him. His father was a horrible crime lord, and his whole life with him was difficult. It's made love such a complicated thing for him."

"Don't be too hard on yourself. I think he does love you. I also think you are right. And it's a difficult thing for him. I think that he hasn't given you the words either."

"He gave me the gesture."

"Trust me, the man is much more likely to jump off

a cliff into the sea than admit his feelings. Don't let him off the hook that easily."

With that, the music changed, and it was their cue to go down the aisle. Andrei was there, standing, his dark eyes glistening with something she couldn't quite discern.

Emotion, maybe. If it were somebody else. But it was Andrei.

And so it was impossible to say.

Did he feel the same way about her?

Would she be able to get it back? If she risked everything. If she tore herself open and bared her heart to him.

She'd already tried. She tried to do it softly. With sweet sex, and he had pushed her away.

So she had to give him the words. She had to.

"And who gives this woman to this man?"

"I do not give her," Onyx said to the priest. "I stand with her, because she is my sister, and I love her. But the choice she makes today is hers. She does not belong to me, nor will she belong to her husband. Princess Emerald will always belong to herself. She stands alone. The most selfless. And I only hope that Andrei understands what he has in her."

Her brother's words were wholly unexpected. They shocked her and brought tears to her eyes.

"Onyx," she said, throwing her arms around his neck and giving him a kiss on the cheek.

She pulled away from him and looked at the front row, where her sister-in-law sat, looking at herself in her front-facing camera.

She wasn't even paying attention to the wedding. Or to the beautiful gesture that her husband had just made.

Circe did not see Onyx. Not for who he really was. Or in any way whatsoever.

She just wanted the crown.

She was a good queen, Emerald could grant her that. She was well loved by the people, and went out of her way to treat everyone with kindness. Except her husband.

But she couldn't fix Onyx's wedding. She also would never be able to forget what he'd said about isolation and loneliness in a marriage.

All she wanted was for her brother to have love.

Worry about yourself.

She found herself being captured by Andrei, his hands large and firm around hers as they stood there in front of the priests. Her whole body was on fire from his touch. Even just last night, he had her. And yet, it would never be enough. But the sex was only a physical expression of the emotion that was already there. It always had been.

Of their desire, of his anger and desperation, of her wordless need for reconciliation and his desperation to take that, even though in the end he had pushed her away.

She needed to add real words to it.

Somehow, she had to show him that they weren't destined to be broken. He was afraid, she thought, not of being his father. But being his mother. Lost in a toxic relationship with a person who didn't care as much as he did. And that was partly her own fault. Or maybe, they were both his mother in a strange way. And somebody had to make the first move.

She already had. It was true. But she would make the first move again and again for him.

Because it had always been him. From the beginning. It would only ever be him.

The words that they spoke in their vows were written by other people, hundreds of years ago, but she did her best to convey everything that they meant to her. To them. This was the one chance she had. This kiss. He had promised her this kiss, and nothing more. So when it was time, she leaned in, and kissed him with everything she had.

She only hoped that he felt it.

What was he? What manner of man, and what father would he be? What manner of husband?

Toxicity? Was that his story. Or was he just resisting vulnerability.

The very idea of it made him choke. She was kissing him, and there was very little else that he wanted in all the world but for Emerald to kiss him. What insanity was he indulging? He had her. She was his wife, and he was holding her at arm's length.

She was right. She had been right all this time. He knew how to want, and he didn't know how to have. And whatever the host of excuses he gave for that, it all came down to fear.

Because love was confusing and terrifying. Because it was both good and bad. Because it hurt, as much as it had ever healed. Because loss was brutal, and when you lost an imperfect person that you loved, you spent all the years after contending with the messy pain of it all.

But he had her. He had her.

So there was nothing left to resist.

He put his hand on her face and he kissed her, poured everything he had into that kiss. Accepted everything she was giving him. It didn't matter what she said. It didn't matter if he loved her more. It didn't matter. Because what was martyrdom, sacrifice, any of it, if it wasn't met with declaration. If it wasn't met with absolute devotion.

His own had been contingent on her actions, and that was weak.

It was the act of a man desperately protecting himself. Maybe she would've chosen another man. Another fate. And so it was up to him to spend the rest of his life proving to her that this was the better path. That this was what they both wanted. He would not do that by shutting her out.

When they parted, she looked dazed, and he felt the same. Their perception was a study in endurance.

He didn't want to be there. He wanted to be alone with her. There were things that needed to be said. But first, he needed to show her that he'd been wrong. About their passion, about their desire: It was so strong that it had the power to encapsulate his rage, his betrayal, and in that moment it had been sharp. But it wasn't toxic. That need between them never could be.

Because he loved her. And if he had to spend the rest of his life working to make her love him in return, then he would.

He would lay it all at her feet.

And finally, when they were able to go back to their suite of rooms, he didn't wait for her to speak. He captured her face in his hands and he kissed her.

"Andrei," she whispered.

"Let me show you," he said.

He would worship her. Her body, her soul. Everything that she was.

He unzipped the back of her dress, and that beautiful creation fell free. He couldn't remember what that ruined wedding dress for her aborted wedding had looked like. Because she had been a bride for him today, and that was all that mattered. Lucian didn't matter. The only way that he mattered was that he had been the catalyst for the two of them finally giving in. For the two of them finally claiming what they actually wanted. For that, he almost had to give thanks for him. Almost.

He would not give the man that much credit.

Underneath the wedding dress was the most beautiful lingerie set he'd ever seen. White, pushing her glorious breasts up, revealing the shadow of her peach-colored nipples beneath. She had white stockings with garters on, and he could see the dusky patch of curls between her thighs, just barely covered by a web of lace.

She was worthy of praise.

She was worthy of everything.

He had thought that fixing his gaze upon a mission would keep his pride intact.

His pride could be damned.

It was nothing. It meant nothing.

"My princess," he said, kneeling before her, an expression of fealty, but so much more. He gripped her hips and pressed his face to that patch of curls between her legs, swept her underwear to the side and began to taste her, lick her. For she was as addictive as any sweet ever could be, and he would never get enough.

She gasped, gripping hold of the back of his head, using it to steady herself. He looked up and saw that her expression was filled with wonder, shock.

Was it love?

In the end, he would make her call out his name, and his alone.

Tonight that might have to be enough.

She came hard, her desire flooding his mouth, and then he kissed his way up her thigh, her hip, her stomach, and kissed her, letting her taste herself on his lips.

When he pulled away, she looked nearly drunk on her own desire.

He knew what had to happen next.

He walked her across the room, brought her to the vanity and bent her over, a repetition of what had happened that night in Alabria.

That night when he had decided to embrace his selfishness.

Affront. That's what it had been. He had been undone by his love for her. Brought to the brink by it. And it was so much easier, so much more comfortable for him to say that he was like his father. Selfish through and through. Because admitting that he loved her, that unmanned him.

And so unmanned was what he would have to be.

He wanted her to see this differently. He gripped her chin, forced her to look straight ahead. "Look at us," he said, his voice tender. He held her throat, softly, letting her feel the care. The strength restrained.

Her breathing was rapid, her pulse fluttering at the base of her throat. He curved his head around and pressed his mouth over it. Kissed her.

And then he unhooked her bra, let her breasts spill free, into his hands, pinched her nipples between his fingers before moving his hands down her hips and tugging her panties down as best he could around the garter belt.

He bent her over, his hand not forceful, but firm. He wanted her to feel the way that he cared about her. The way that he held her.

He wanted her to feel the shift, the promise.

"Look at us," he whispered.

He wrapped her hair around his hand and breathed in deeply, the scent of lilacs and summertime. Of Emerald.

He freed himself from his briefs, and pushed deep inside her. He held them both there, like that, an expression of awe and wonder on her face, one that was matched on his own. "I love you," he growled.

He thrust forward, claiming her, over and over again, driving them both to the brink. "I love you," he said.

"I love you."

He said it with each thrust. Like a prayer, like a promise. He said it from the very depths of himself. Because it was true, whether she ever said it to him or not. Because that was what it had always been. And yes, he had loved her with the promise of never having her in return, and there was something about that that had comforted him. Because he had been a boy, scared, of his own memories, of himself, but he wasn't afraid anymore. He had thought that this was being unmanned. That wasn't true.

His father was not a man. Because he had never truly been able to love those around him more than he loved his own pride, his own comfort, himself.

But Andrei loved her. More than anything.

He lost his control then, on a shout, pouring himself into her as she lost her own control, gripping the edge of the vanity, trembling and shaking.

"Andrei," she whispered, his name a sob, and when she looked back up at him in the mirror, their body still joined, there were tears on her face.

He withdrew from her, turning her to face him and cupping her. "Did I hurt you?"

"No. You love me?"

"Yes. I love you. And I am sorry that I didn't tell you before. I was afraid. I was afraid of what it meant to be in love with you alone."

"You're not," she said. "I promise you that you're not. I love you. I… I was going to tell you this tonight. I wanted us to have a wedding night too. I swear it. I was going to keep giving myself to you, throwing myself at you until you believed it. But I knew that I needed to give you the words. The reason that I went ahead with the wedding to Lucian was because I was scared. Not of what he would do, but of my feelings for you. What I accused you of, that was me. I was so comfortable pining for you." She swallowed hard. "I told my brother that the reason I couldn't be with you because you weren't royal. He reminded me that he never would've cared. I knew that." She choked on a sob. "I knew that. It was never why. It was always because I feared that if I had you, I would love you in such a way that I would lose myself, and Andrei, I struggle… Even with the memory of my mother."

She buried her face in his neck, crying in earnest now, and he simply held her. "The reason that it has to be a mission is because if it's not, then she's just someone that I miss. And I miss her so much. Every day. I remember when she died, and she'd been gone a week, that it was the longest I'd ever been away from her. And every day… It's the longest I've ever been away from her. And time just keeps going on, but the pain doesn't go away. So it's better to turn it into action. And then there was you." She looked up at him. "I loved you from the first moment I saw you. And it was a relief, because I knew that I couldn't marry someone who wasn't a king or prince. Don't you see, it protected me from everything. Making my mother's memory a crusade. It kept me from grieving her, and it kept me from being hurt by you. But what I didn't anticipate was that our feelings were just too strong for that. It broke down my walls. It broke down all of my defenses."

"Emerald," he whispered. "My princess. You broke down all of mine. I have never wanted anyone else. Not really. I've never loved another. And you are right.

There was something deeply comforting in that. But I think we know how to love each other. We have worked together, helped each other. We have passion. We have friendship. Over every stage in our relationship, we have found these things, and now all that is left for us is to put them together. As husband and wife. As parents. Lovers. Friends."

"Yes," she whispered.

Here they were, newly married, half naked, and filled with love for one another. "I can't wait to tell Onyx."

He laughed. "Maybe he will be my friend again."

"He better be. You are, after all, going to be the father of his very first niece or nephew. And you are his brother-in-law now."

"And we are family," he whispered.

"Yes. Forever."

EPILOGUE

When Honora Rose was born, named for her two grandmothers that she would never know, no one was happier than her mother and father.

Though her uncle was close behind them.

Onyx held his precious niece, and smiled up at Emerald. "Thank God she favors you. If she had looked like Andrei…"

"A pity," Andrei said. "That she is so brilliantly ginger like her mother, only because that is part of how I convinced Lucian to extricate himself from the situation."

Onyx laughed. It was all funny now.

His relationship with Andrei had repaired itself fairly quickly after the wedding. He had seen how happy Andrei and Emerald were together, and he couldn't stay angry.

The issue really had always been the violation of his trust, but once he realized how wrecked Andrei and Emerald had been over the whole thing, how much they had hurt each other in the process, he hadn't felt like he had the right to stay angry.

"You are ready to be a father," Emerald said.

"Yes," Onyx agreed. "It is time for me to have an heir. I… Circe and I have been discussing it. I… It's time."

She felt bad, but the idea of her brother being even more tied to his wife than he already was made her feel sick for him. That was silly, she supposed. They were married.

But he wasn't happy.

She could only hope that the addition of a child to her brother's marriage would do something to break the wall of ice between the spouses. But she had her doubts.

Then again, she and Andrei had found their way to each other. After everything.

After Onyx left their quarters, it was time for Honora to have her nap, and Emerald lay down in the bed holding the baby, with Andrei beside her. This was what she had always imagined was impossible. This happiness. The simple joy.

This was what Emerald, the woman, not the princess, not the symbol, had always wanted. This sweet, simple happiness with the man she loved.

She smiled.

"What?"

"Oh, I was just thinking. Love is so simple. When you can heal from all the things that kept you captive all your life."

Andrei laughed. "Yes. Such a simple thing. And a miracle."

He leaned in and kissed her, and she had never been

so grateful. For everything. Even the pain. Because it had brought them here.

And there was nowhere else she would rather be.

* * * * *

If you just couldn't get enough of
Princess, Pregnant, Prisoner,
then be sure to check out King's Captive Bride,
the next installment in the
Young, Hot and Royal trilogy by Millie Adams!

And why not explore these other stories
by Millie Adams?

His Highness's Diamond Decree
After-Hours Heir
Dragos's Broken Vows
Promoted to Boss's Wife
Heir of Scandal

Available now!